You'

You have a baby due in a month.

The last thing you need is to feel like this.

About your landlord.

Your sexy, manly, capable, laid-back landlord.

She made a frustrated sound, and it seemed to make him stir. She was just about to whisper something to him about getting to bed—he could stay on the couch till morning, if he wanted, but she needed her room—when he reached out.

Was he still asleep?

His hand curved around the back of her head and pulled her closer. His eyes were still closed. His nose nudged forward. Where was the mouth he was looking for? Ahh…

His lips were so warm. She had to drag herself away. She had to! Or push him, or tell him, "Wake up, Andy. I'm not whoever you think I am."

But none of that happened. She let him kiss her, her own mouth motionless while his lips coaxed her. He mumbled, "Mmm," the sound coming from deep in his chest. He wanted a response. His dream self was growing frustrated that these soft lips beneath his weren't answering the kiss.

How could she answer it?

How could she *not*?

Dear Reader,

I'm lucky enough to be part of a wonderful group of writers who go away together once a year for an intensive week of writing, brainstorming and craft discussion. Okay, I admit there is a small and responsible amount of eating, laughing and drinking, as well.

During a brainstorming session, one of our group was looking for inspiration for her next series and I came up with a great idea for a trilogy featuring a family of successful doctors. There was the high-achieving older brother, the laid-back middle child, the burned-out younger sister. I threw in a beautiful rural setting, a baby or two and a couple of characters—a gold-digging blonde and a blue-collar cop—whom you wouldn't necessarily expect to be the best match for the hero or heroine concerned. I was so inspired about it…and my friend wasn't interested.

Writing is funny that way. What sets off fireworks of inspiration for one writer will leave another writer totally cold. "Would you mind if I kept the idea, then?" I asked her. Trust me, she wasn't planning to fight me for it. Undeterred by her lack of enthusiasm, I rushed back to my room with the whole thing fizzing and singing in my head, and started writing until my hand hurt.

Two hours later I had the basic outline for the three stories that would become the McKinley Medics trilogy, and now here's the first book. *Daddy on Her Doorstep* is Andy's story, and who better to pair with a laid-back rural doctor than an uptight city woman with endearingly rigid ideas about having a baby on her own? I hope you enjoy Andy and Claudia's journey, and that you'll look out for *A Doctor in His House,* coming in May 2012.

Lilian Darcy

DADDY ON
HER DOORSTEP

LILIAN DARCY

SPECIAL EDITION

Recycling programs
for this product may
not exist in your area.

ISBN-13: 978-0-373-65658-5

DADDY ON HER DOORSTEP

Printed in U.S.A.

Books by Lilian Darcy

Harlequin Special Edition

The Mommy Miracle #2134
**Daddy on Her Doorstep* #2176

Silhouette Special Edition

Balancing Act #1552
Their Baby Miracle #1672
The Father Factor #1696
†*The Runaway and
  the Cattleman* #1762
†*Princess in Disguise* #1766
†*Outback Baby* #1774
The Couple Most Likely To #1801
A Mother in the Making #1880
The Millionaire's Makeover #1899
The heiress's Baby #2063

Silhouette Romance

The Baby Bond #1390
Her Sister's Child #1449
Raising Baby Jane #1478
Cinderella After Midnight #1542
Saving Cinderella #1555
Finding Her Prince #1567
Pregnant and Protected #1603
For the Taking #1620
The Boss's Baby Surprise #1729
The Millionaire's Cinderella Wife #1772
Sister Swap #1816

Family Secrets

Racing Hearts

†Wanted: Outback Wives
*The Cinderella Conspiracy
**McKinley Medics

Other titles by Lilian Darcy
available in ebook format.

LILIAN DARCY

has written nearly eighty books for Silhouette Romance, Special Edition and Harlequin Medical Romance (Prescription Romance). Happily married, with four active children and a very patient cat, she enjoys keeping busy and could probably fill several more lifetimes with the things she likes to do—including cooking, gardening, quilting, drawing and traveling. She currently lives in Australia but travels to the United States as often as possible to visit family. Lilian loves to hear from readers. You can write to her at P.O. Box 532, Jamison P.O., Macquarie ACT 2614, Australia, or email her at lilian@liliandarcy.com.

Chapter One

Pregnant.

Andy's new tenant hadn't mentioned that little detail over the phone. He sat at the wheel of his pickup and watched her unloading her things onto the porch, with a vague sense that he was spying, while he gave about thirty percent of his attention to his sister Scarlett's voice in his ear. "...so there was nothing we could do, and it was so fast..."

A very nice wheeled designer suitcase thumped up the wooden steps. The new tenant paused to stretch her lower back, placing a hand there for support.

The bump of her pregnancy was unmistakable in this pose, neat and round and firm, but as soon as she straightened again it almost disappeared. She had the kind of long, lean, gym-honed body that made a pregnancy look like this season's hot fashion accessory, and she was probably a little chilly in those three-quarter-length sleeves, since it was only the beginning of April and the clear air had a definite bite.

"...so I've been thinking I might take a week off, just some quiet time, but not here in the city..." Scarlett had called Andy on his cell just as he was about to drive past his own house on his way from his office to the store, so he'd pulled over in front of his neighbor's place to take her call, only a few yards from his own driveway. He hadn't intended to watch his new tenant unloading her car, it had just happened that way.

"...and if it wouldn't create problems for you and Laura..." he heard Scarlett say into his ear.

He put his reply in fast. "Laura and I have split up."

"Oh, Andy! When?" His sister sounded distressed.

"February. It's okay. It's not a problem."

There was a beat of silence as Scarlett absorbed the news. "She tried too hard, didn't she?"

"Yeah, she did," he admitted, glad that Scarlett understood, so he didn't have to explain.

"Was she upset?"

"She was the one who made the move. I came home from work and there was a note and a whole lot less stuff." The extent of Laura's stuff had been part of the problem. "But we both knew it was coming. She's found someone who appreciates her for who she truly is, the note said."

"Ouch!"

"And she was right. I really didn't do that."

Speaking of ouch...

The tenant heaved a second suitcase out of the trunk of her car and paused once again to arch and rub away the ache in her back. Her outfit looked brand-new and designer label, the soft sage-green stretch fabric gathered at the side seams so that it made her bump into a graceful curve instead of an inconvenient bulge.

Her dark brown hair shone with rich chestnut lights, and the artfully casual topknot looked as if it had been twisted and pinned in place at a Manhattan salon not more than half an hour ago, just as the fringed and patterned scarf around her neck could have been draped by a Hollywood stylist. Her sunglasses said *expensive* loud and clear.

But it was the bump that had him thinking.

"Definitely pregnant," Andy muttered. "Wonder when she's due…"

"Sorry?" said Scarlett.

"My new tenant seems to be pregnant."

"Oh, you have a new tenant? Ohh…"

He couldn't miss the disappointment. "Is that a problem?"

Seemed to be the tenant that was the problem for his sister, not the pregnancy. He didn't have a problem with either the tenant or her fashionable bump, but he was a little curious about why a woman like this—all big-city sophistication and style—was here in a small, scenic town in Vermont, renting solo, on a short-term lease. Where did the pregnancy fit in?

"Well, see, that's what I've been working up to," Scarlett said. "I'm taking some time off. Hoping to. Thinking about it. I'd been wondering if I could use your rental half, since it's been empty. You know, just sit in a porch swing for a week."

"You can sit in my porch swing, instead of the rental one."

"I know, but it's not the same."

"It's almost the same," he pointed out, "since my place and my rental are two halves of the same house."

He'd loved the extravagant Victorian on sight, four years ago, and since he hadn't needed such a big place, he'd been happy that it was divided into two generous apartments. He was casual about renting out the half he didn't live in, relying on word of mouth and a couple of low-key listings on the internet, preferring short leases for the variety. He hadn't hugely cared when it stood vacant, as it had been all this past winter, while his two-year relationship with Laura had done its slow, splintering crash, like a felled tree.

"Yeah, but that's… No, I can't explain." Scarlett sounded very flat, and very tired.

"This is only a three-month rental," he began.

This was what made him curious. Three months renting to a pregnant tenant from New York City, who had most definitely told him on the phone that she'd be living there alone, and that she didn't want a longer lease because she was only subletting her condo in Manhattan for the first two months, and didn't want it sitting empty for too long. She was a corporate accountant, she'd said.

So where did her due date fit in to her stay here? What was her plan? What were her intentions once the three-month lease was up?

"So if I hold off on my vacation until July…" Scarlett said.

"You may actually be able to come up here and get a Vermont tan," he finished for her. "And make it longer than a week. Make it as long as you want."

He'd experienced for himself the therapeutic benefits of escaping the city and coming to the Green Mountain state. Five and a half years ago, one weekend here had led to a major change of lifestyle and priorities. Scarlett had been largely responsible for the whole thing, and now he had a chance to return the favor.

"But, no, I'll never get July," she said. "New rotations start. I have a shot at August. Just a week…" She was talking to herself more than to him, mentally adjusting her heavy schedule.

Like every member of the McKinley family except Andy, she was all about crammed schedules. He remembered all too well what that was like.

On the porch, a heavy-looking cardboard box was about to join the two suitcases. This time, the arch-and-rub was followed by a hard lean onto the seat of the porch swing. The swing rocked too much and the pregnant tenant…Nelson, Claudia Nelson…almost lost her balance. She grabbed the swing chain, pivoted on one foot and sat on the moving seat with a hard thump, and Andy had to fight an impulse to leap out of the pickup and rush to her aid.

Which she might not have appreciated, since she would have no idea who he was at this point. Anyhow, she'd recovered her balance now.

Recovered her balance, but not her built-in cool. She flattened her hand over her upper chest and took some breaths that looked as if they'd been learned in prenatal class and practiced diligently since. In through the nose. Out slow and steady, through rounded lips.

Shoot, she wasn't in labor, was she? She only looked around six months or so, but as he'd already observed, she had the kind of body where it was hard to tell.

"I'd better go," he told Scarlett. "Think about it for August or whenever, and call me back when you decide. Please."

"I will."

"I'll hold off on another tenant for a while when this

one moves out. Meanwhile, if you want to come up sooner, I can check out some of the bed-and-breakfasts around here. They're pretty quiet. And I can make sure a porch swing is part of the deal."

"Thanks, Andy. But, no, it was probably a dumb idea." Down the line, Scarlett sighed to herself and began planning again. "I'll wait. Even August, with the new interns... I'll check the calendar. Maybe October..."

Scarlett disconnected the call before Andy could tell her that October sounded too far off, given the stress and fatigue in her voice. He knew what his father, Dr. Michael James McKinley, Senior, would have said to her: "Get a good night's sleep and pull yourself together, Scarlett. You're a cancer specialist. You're going to lose patients. You can't let it get too personal."

Speaking of personal, it was time for Andy to introduce himself to the lady with the bump. The trip to the store for some steak and potatoes to accompany salad and a beer as tonight's meal would have to wait.

There was a man in the front yard. Claudia had been vaguely aware of him since he'd pulled to the curb thirty feet down the street to take a call on his cell, but then she'd taken her eye off him for a few moments while she caught her breath after that scary near-fall.

Now, instead of ending the call and driving away as she would have expected, he was suddenly here, coming toward her, smiling as if he knew her.

Or as if he had suspect intentions.

She had a moment of vulnerability, unfamiliar and unwanted. The baby crammed itself against her lungs, making her breath short. Her female friends—well, her one best friend, Kelly, plus her work colleagues and her hair stylist—kept telling her approvingly that she barely showed. But, oh, the baby was there, and if she didn't show much from the outside it was only because the pregnancy was crowding out her internal organs, instead.

What did this man want? Around her own age of thirty-four, he looked strong and competent and sure of himself, dark haired, square-jawed, crooked-nosed, dressed in conservative dark pants and a pale polo shirt, with sleeve bands that stretched tight around hard biceps. His stride was long and he had an aura of casual ownership.

Of the moment.

Of the situation.

It might have been appealing in other circumstances. She liked competence and control in a man.

Right now, however, there was no traffic going by and the air had filled with an odd stillness, as if she and this stranger were the only two people anywhere near. He was kind of frowning and smiling at her at the same time. He was incredibly good-looking, with an especially nice mouth. Any woman would be bound to notice. But he was big and strong and she was no match for him physically. Especially not now.

She stood, and the swing rocked again, reminding her of how she'd almost fallen a moment ago, and then had bumped down on it painfully hard.

Scary. Unsettling.

She was used to grace and strength in her body, not this clumsiness.

She was used to being fully in control.

She wasn't used to this instinctive gesture of curving one hand in protection across her lower stomach, while the other was pressed against her beating heart.

I want this baby, she reminded herself. *I chose it. I went for it. It was a considered decision after a ton of research and planning. I didn't sit around whining that there weren't any good men and that my body clock was ticking.*

She wanted the baby, yes, but she wasn't a huge fan of the actual pregnancy. It made her feel caged and vulnerable, a familiar feeling from long ago that she hated and fought or avoided whenever she could.

"Claudia?" the stranger said, still with the frown and the grin.

"Y-yes?" He'd said her *name.*

"Hi. It's nice to meet you." He held out his hand, showing strong, clean fingers. "I'm your landlord. Andy McKinley."

Her landlord! Sheesh, of course he was! *Claudia, you panicky idiot!* She even recognized his gravelly voice from the phone.

Oh, shoot, she was going to cry.

I'm not. I'm not.

This was another thing she didn't love about the pregnancy—all the hormonal emotions sloshing around inside her. Just the switch from slight—and let's face it, pretty irrational—fear about a stranger's approach to relief that he had a good reason for smiling at her, knowing her name and giving off that sense of ownership, was enough to dampen her eyes and tighten her throat.

"Nice to meet you, too," she managed, after swallowing the tears back. Fortunately, she was still wearing her driving sunglasses so he wouldn't have seen. She took her hand away from her chest, returned his handshake and found her fingers engulfed in a warmth and strength that once again reminded her of her own new vulnerability. "I'm a little earlier than I said."

"No problem."

"Um, Mr. McKinley, how come you're parked in the street, not turned into the driveway?"

"I was on my way to the store when my sister called, so I pulled over."

"Oh, right. It...uh...threw me a little, when you came across the grass. I didn't know who you could be."

"Yeah, I can see how you could get the wrong idea. Sorry about that."

"It's fine. Just wanted to explain. I don't normally react like a deer in the headlights when a perfectly respectable man says hello to me."

"Good to know." He gave another smile-and-frown, kind of crooked, and she felt she still hadn't been fully on message. *I'm not a jittery flake, I'm on top of everything I do.* But if she didn't let it go at this point, she would only make things worse. "And it's Dr. McKinley, if you want to get technical."

"Oh. Dr. McKinley. Okay."

"Let me help you get your things inside and show you around," he said easily. "I saw you lose your balance on the swing just now. Are you okay?" He stepped closer.

"I'm fine," she said firmly.

"Sure?"

"Quite sure." What did he want from her? He was still studying her, frowning. If only he would look away, she might just rub her lower back again because it ached so much from the drive and the hefting of baggage. She didn't want to rub it while he was watching, because even now that she knew who he was, she didn't want to telegraph the vulnerability she disliked so much.

She could still hear her mother's voice on the subject

of the baby, still see her openly scathing expression. *Are you crazy?* The words had come out harsh and strident and a little fuzzy after several glasses of good wine. *Doing it on your own, by choice?* There'd still been a wineglass in Mom's hand as she spoke, held very gracefully by its slender crystal stem but threatening to spill. *Do you have any idea? It's nothing like getting a degree or taking the partnership track, Claudia.*

Just as getting through a bottle or two of French chardonnay or very nice Australian shiraz every night in the privacy of her own home, while wearing expensive jewelry and glittery clothes, was nothing like being an alcoholic, in Mom's view.

Claudia's argument that she was thirty-four years old, she was a highly competent professional with a corner office that she'd well and truly earned, she was financially secure, she was dealing in a sensible, practical way with the fact that there seemed to be *zero* decent available men in New York City and she had thought her decision through with enormous care and a detailed budget, hadn't swayed her mother's opinion one jot. "You'll find you've bitten off way more than you can chew, my girl."

Forget about it, Claudia, she lectured herself now, *it was months ago.*

But darn it, she just couldn't help rubbing her back, and Andy McKinley had seen.

"I'll just mention," he said carefully, "that I'm a family practitioner, with a sub-specialty in ob-gyn." He took a key ring from his pocket.

"I'm not due for five and a half weeks. And since first babies are often late, I'm working on six."

"Mmm, so you are planning to have the baby here

in Vermont?" He unlocked her front door, extended the handles on her suitcases and wheeled them both into the front hallway. He had strong wrists with a tan line on them that suggested he liked to ski.

"That's right." She explained briefly in what she privately called her spreadsheet voice, "I wanted a calm atmosphere for the last weeks of the pregnancy, and for the birth. I wanted my body to recover and to get our bonding and our routine in place in peace and quiet for six weeks or so before I go back to the city and then to work."

"So you're going back to work...?"

"When the baby is three months old. I'll spend my last six weeks of maternity leave back in the city, getting systems in place. I've already researched nanny agencies and I'm on the books of the best one in the city," she said, then added so that he wasn't left in any doubt, "I'm going to be a single parent. I'll just say it up front. This was a planned pregnancy, using a sperm-donor father, at a highly reputable Manhattan clinic."

"Got you."

"It's good to get these things out in the open, I think, rather than have you wondering, and making things embarrassing for both of us." She smiled, again making it brief and cool to give him his cue.

"Right," he said, nodding and smiling back. Again it was a little crooked, she noticed. As if his view of the world was a complicated thing. As if he stood back from life, faintly amused by the whole messy business. "Thanks for filling me in."

"Well, it doesn't make sense not to."

"Six weeks before, six weeks after. I guess that about takes care of your three-month lease." He sounded cheerful about it, but maybe she was a little defensive after her mother's often-repeated refrain of, *You're crazy.* She thought she detected some hidden...what?... Criticism? Skepticism? Amusement?

All three.

Why did people have so much trouble believing that a pregnant woman could be organized? That a single-by-choice mother could make good decisions? That even *being* a single-by-choice mother was a good decision? That proper planning and budgeting did actually lead to a more successful outcome, and babies on a solid routine were more content? It was basic common sense!

And why did people think it was any of their business, even if they did happen to be doctors who knew about babies?

"There's no need to show me around," she told him, cool about it once again. "I've seen your photo tour on the internet and I'm confident there's everything I'll need. As long as the furnace is hot and the refrigerator is cold?"

"Checked them both this morning."

"Great. Thanks."

"I'll bring your boxes in."

She would have argued, but her back told her not to, so she simply thanked him again, gritted her teeth and waited until he'd shunted the remaining two boxes inside.

"Want me to take those suitcases up?"

"Thanks, no, I'll be fine."

"I'll leave you to it, then. I'm right next door, if there's anything you need."

"The nearest store?"

"Straight on down the street, make a left at the end,

then a right on Route 11, and you'll hit a shopping plaza on your left in about half a mile."

"Thanks."

"You're welcome." He gave a casual click of his tongue in farewell and sloped off along the porch to his own front door. Was he *whistling?*

He didn't seem like any doctor she'd met before. Nothing like the rather stuffy, fifty-something, highly recommended and very expensive ob-gyn she'd been seeing in Manhattan. More like a rancher with that pickup he'd climbed out of.

If you went by the whistle, he was Tom Sawyer, all grown up. If you went by the crooked nose, someone who'd had a minor accident while skiing or climbing, or even a punch-up outside a bar. Or maybe a construction-crew boss. Someone who knew what he was doing, but was laid-back about it. Someone good with his hands and with tools.

This place, for example. Had he remodeled it himself?

It was beautiful. The internet tour hadn't given a misleading impression. Late afternoon spring sunshine poured through the kitchen window on the first floor and her bedroom window above. The wide bay window at the side of the house would glow when the morning sun hit those leaded sections of stained glass.

Beyond the borders of a Persian rug, the hardwood floors shone a dark syrup color, and the two couches looked soft and inviting with their stylized floral fabric. There were prints on the walls, wrought-iron fire tongs on a stand beside the grate, a good-quality coffee table and end tables made of solid wood, thick cream drapes at the windows for privacy, carved newel posts and rails on the stairs.

For the moment, however, with the baby kicking and rolling in a very uncomfortable way, the most urgent piece of exploration she needed was to check out the state of the bathroom.

Of course, Andy ran into her at the supermarket on the outskirts of town less than forty-five minutes later.

She was efficient, he'd give her that. She'd asked for directions to the store, and in the time he'd taken to unwind in a lazy, casual way from a day of seeing patients with conditions ranging from ingrown toenails to advanced pregnancy to serious heart disease, she'd—he could hear her faintly through the walls—toured both levels of the half a Victorian house that were now temporarily hers, tested the bathroom facilities, unpacked at least one of the suitcases and taken a long and no doubt critical look from the back porch at a garden he hadn't touched since last summer.

Now she was shopping, arriving at the spacious, brightly lit supermarket just off County Route 5 only a few minutes after he'd gotten here himself.

He had steak, potatoes, orange juice and bananas in his basket.

She was filling a whole cart, stocking up big-time.

Buying diapers already?

He had to smile. Of course she was buying diapers!

He'd pegged her to a T, in the space of just a few minutes of conversation. He'd met her kind before. A highly intelligent and competent city professional, who would sincerely believe that efficiently stocking up six weeks in advance on non-perishable baby supplies would give her a significant head start in acquiring that all-important "routine" that would miraculously turn the years-long demands of parenthood, whether solo or shared, into a walk in the park.

Boy, was she in for a shock.

It was funny…

And not.

He didn't know what to feel, actually.

Impressed? It was brave, no doubt about that. Angry? He was so busy with this mix of wry amusement, anger and…something else that he couldn't quite work out… that he forgot to keep track of her movements through the store and found her coming down the dairy aisle toward him, pausing to reach for yogurt and cheese on the way.

"Oh. Hi," she said.

And caught him looking at the stack of diapers.

He hadn't meant to, but they were hard to miss—five big, block-shaped, plastic-covered, newborn-size sixty-packs piled one on top of the other.

Ten diapers a day for a month. Seven a day for six weeks. Take your pick. She'd probably already worked out a theoretical schedule for how often the baby would need changing.

She flushed. "It's not like they'll spoil. This way, I get to carry them into the house while I'm not too big and not too sore."

"Makes sense," he agreed.

And it kind of did. Of course it was a good idea to get as much done in advance as you could. But it was a drop in the ocean.

They stood there, him with the basket hooked over his arm, her leaning on the piled-up cart. Her hair was gleaming and pretty but a little too tightly wound for his taste. He liked fullness and bounce, soft waves shadowing a woman's face, something to run his fingers through, something to tickle his shoulders or cheeks or chest when he came in for a kiss. Was the tight style another piece of efficiency on her part?

Knot it and go. Nothing to get in the way.

She was incredibly well-groomed close up, even more so than he'd observed when he'd first seen her on the porch. Soft hands, their long fingers tipped with a French manicure. Neat gold earrings with just the right amount of sparkle and dangle. A touch of lip gloss. Perfectly arched eyebrows with not a hair out of line. Low-heeled ankle boots and that artfully arranged scarf.

And what was the deal with the scarf, anyhow? If he had something like that fussing around his neck, it would either choke him or fall off every time he moved. It'd drive him crazy. She carried it with casual grace. He wondered if he was underestimating her and she would soon carry a baby on her hip the same way.

Due in five and a half weeks. First babies weren't *always* late.

Would she manage on her own? Did she have support systems in place that she hadn't mentioned yet?

I'm going to find out...

A danger signal suddenly clanged in his head. His father had accused him in the past of being a soft touch for people in need. *You don't know how to keep your distance, Andy. When you let yourself get overinvolved, all that happens is mess and complication.*

Was Dad right? He often asked himself this, because Dad was right about a lot of things and knew it. He was a heart surgeon, and patients came to him from hundreds of miles away. But was he right that Andy had a tendency to become overinvolved?

The question hung in the balance for what felt like too long. He murmured something polite in Claudia

Nelson's direction. *See you back at the house. Good luck with your shopping.* The words didn't matter. He was only using them as an exit line. Then he moved on down the aisle.

But when he turned at the end, remembering he needed to pick up some milk, he looked toward her, saw her pick up several cans of tomatoes from a lower shelf and once more straighten and rub the band of tightness around her lower back. Suddenly, she looked far too alone, marooned in the middle of a brightly lit supermarket aisle in her designer maternity clothes.

"She's not going to go five more weeks..." he muttered to himself in a flash of medical intuition. "One or two if she's lucky. A couple of days if she keeps on with the superwoman stuff."

Trying to look casual about it, he wandered back. "Hey, I've just thought, would you like to come next door for dinner tonight, since you've had a full day? Save you calling out for pizza?"

"I wasn't calling out for pizza, I was going to cook."

Of course she was going to cook!

"Save you cooking, even better," he said, keeping it cheerful and bland. "It's only going to be steak and green salad and microwaved potatoes."

"Well, the baby does need iron," she murmured, half to herself, frowning as if working out complex numbers in her head. "But for vitamins, just a green salad...?"

Andy hid another smile. She probably calculated her nutritional intake on a daily basis. He shouldn't laugh about it, when this was so much better than the patients he saw who paid no attention to their nutrition during pregnancy at all. "Will an offer of broccoli on the side seal the deal? Fresh fruit for dessert?"

Reading his attitude, she fixed him with a patient,

tolerant expression, and drawled, "Organic? Locally grown?"

"Great. We're on the same page." And she had a sense of humor, even if she was a trifle scary.

"What time shall I come over?" she asked.

"Six? I don't want to keep you late."

"Six sounds good."

They parted company and he went to the produce section and lost his head a little, throwing into his basket broccoli, cherry tomatoes, mushrooms, mangoes, purple onion, baby spinach, parsley, carrots, strawberries and corn.

Standing at the checkout, he looked at the crowded plastic basket and clicked his tongue. His father was right. Ten different items from the fruit and vegetable group was definitely overinvolved.

Chapter Two

Andy heard Claudia's neat knock at his front door at five after six, when he had the electric grill heating up, the broccoli and corn in the steamer, the potatoes circling in the microwave and the colorful salad already tossed in the bowl.

He'd even cooked up the mushrooms, parsley and onions to make a gravy for the steak, and the mangoes and strawberries sat on the table in another bowl ready to serve as dessert, little cubes of orange and blobs of red.

His new tenant wanted nutrition and she was going to get it, with bells on.

She seemed a little edgy after she'd followed him into the kitchen and looked at what he had on the table and stove top. "You're doing all this for me?"

"I'm a doctor, remember? I totally support women eating well during pregnancy."

"Thank you." *But you still think I'm nuts.*

She didn't say it, but she looked at him, head tilted a little, and he could read her face.

Or rather her chin and her eyes.

The chin was raised, showing her lovely, streamlined jaw. Her eyes were narrowed in a mix of defiance and uneasiness. The dark, gleaming knot still sat tight on the top of her head. She was pretty sure of herself with this planned solo pregnancy thing, and yet something—or someone—had put some doubts in her mind at some point.

"No problems with your half of the house so far?" he asked, throwing the steaks onto the grill.

"No, it's beautiful, a great environment, a wonderful sense of peace and space and light, just what I was looking for. And the town is lovely."

"What else are you looking for?" he asked before stopping to consider what a personal question it was. He added quickly, "Here in Radford, I mean." The addition made his query somewhat more acceptable.

"Well, I've chosen the Spring Ridge Memorial Hospital for the birth, if that's what you mean."

"Mitchum Medical Center is closer." Radford itself was too small to warrant a hospital.

"Mitchum didn't have the high-level neonatal facilities I was looking for. Not that I expect to need them."

"Still, it's a good hospital." He sent patients there all the time, delivered most of his babies there.

"Oh, I'm sure it is. I wasn't implying—"

"It's fine. Just wanted you to know there is a good hospital ten minutes from here."

"An hour to Spring Ridge isn't that far."

"They have an excellent neonatal transport team, if a baby has to be moved."

"Don't they say it's always better to move a baby when it's still inside the mom?"

Were they arguing?

She seemed to realize it, too, and pulled back from her defensive position. "As you point out, though, ten minutes is closer. I'll take your advice and look at Mitchum Medical. Maybe it's not too late to book in there, if it has everything on my checklist." There was a tiny pause, then she added, "It's so good of you to have me over. I wasn't expecting that from a landlord. Can I put plates on the table? How can I help?"

He directed her to the crockery and silverware, and she went out and laid them on the formal dining table that he almost never used, when he'd envisaged eating here in the kitchen. The choice seemed typical of the differences between them. She liked structure, he was laid-back. She preferred planning, he liked to go with the flow. She dressed for dinner, he stayed in his jeans.

And, in fact, she seriously had changed outfits, he registered. This ensemble was green, like the outfit she'd been wearing earlier, but the green was a little darker, the fabric silkier, and instead of one stretchy top, she wore some kind of tank or T-shirt or blouse with a matching jacket on top. It would probably appall her to learn that he'd taken this long to notice the difference.

It might appall her even more to know that he was struggling not to notice other things. The fineness of her skin. The way she smelled. The mix of lean grace and pregnant clumsiness in how she moved. He was appalled about it, himself. This was not the kind of over-involvement Dad talked about. It was worse.

They sat down to eat, and asked each other the usual polite questions. Do you have family in the area? You must enjoy your work?

Her answers were almost the same as his. She loved her career. She had family in New York City.

"Although it's really just my mom," she said. "My parents divorced a long time ago, and I'm an only child. My dad's still in Allentown."

"Pennsylvania?"

"That's right. I'm not sure what Billy Joel was thinking, setting a song there. There is *nothing* romantic or interesting about Allentown! And I was born there, so I'm allowed to say it." She wasn't smiling. Sounded almost angry about it, as if she and Allentown had been through a bitter and drawn-out breakup.

Well, maybe in a way they had...

"Your dad likes it, though," he pointed out gently, with some sympathy for the unknown man who'd chosen to remain in a small working-class city on a pretty river, instead of moving into the fast lanes of Philadelphia or New York.

"He must." *Don't go there,* said her tone and her elbows, pinching in at her sides, making her shoulders and whole body look tense.

Andy wanted to tell her to lighten up. He wanted to tease her or tell jokes until she smiled. His sister Scarlett was like this, so driven and rigid. He'd been like this once himself. Successful but unhappy and riding for a fall and not even knowing it. He scrambled for something to say, finding inspiration in the way the silky fabric of her jacket caught the light. "Some of my pregnant patients will want to know where you get your maternity clothes."

"Oh!" She beamed suddenly, and the wide smile softened her whole face. "You think?" For a moment she'd lost the stiffness and narrow control, and the difference in her seemed to light up the whole room. "I do love this outfit!"

She ran her fingers lightly down the sides of the jacket, unconsciously emphasizing breasts made fuller by pregnancy. Then she straightened the neckline of the top beneath and Andy felt an unwanted—and unwarranted—tightening in his groin. She had such graceful, sexy hands, all smooth skin and long fingers and neat nails. And to watch her touching herself in unconscious sensuality...

But she was his tenant, and she was pregnant, and the baby had a file number in a fertility clinic for a father, and he wasn't going anywhere near any of that. Dad would be proud. He chewed some steak, instead.

"Clothes are so important," she said, still energized by the subject. "Well, to me. I love beautiful cuts and colors and fabrics. And you're right, it's hard to find nice things when you're pregnant. I researched it early on, and put together a whole list, stores and catalogs and online, grouped by price range. I could print it out if you think your patients might find it helpful. It would be no trouble."

So she had a streak of kindness and an appreciation of beauty, along with the rigidity and cool-headed efficiency and drive...

"Really?" he said. "You would?"

"Of course, or I wouldn't have said it."

"I might take you up on that. I'll ask our practice nurse, Annette. Some patients do ask her about that kind of thing."

"And does Annette have time to answer? I found in Manhattan it was all such a rush. Sit on this bench and have blood taken. Sit at that desk and fill out the questionnaire. I'm hoping it's a little more personal up here."

"It's probably less efficient, though, I should warn you."

"I can do efficiency on my own." The crispness was back. "From my obstetrician I need time and attention and openness to the needs of a first-time, single-by-choice mom. If I've taken the trouble to write down my questions in advance, I expect a doctor or nurse to take the trouble to give me answers."

"You're not wrong…"

"No. But you'd be surprised. People act as if there's some mysterious, floating magic about having a baby. There's not." She was indignant, fluent, still energized. "I've done my reading, I have my birth plan in place, my labor partner Kelly is on standby. She's my best friend, newly married and hoping to be a mom within a year or two herself, and she's been at the classes with me. She's coming up here a week in advance of the birth. She's giving me a portable crib as her gift for the baby, bringing it when she comes."

"Very practical," he agreed. As long as the baby co-operated and came at the right time.

"I heard from her this afternoon and it was delivered to her place today. We researched all the available models together and chose the best one. In fact, I've researched everything I could, and I'm not going to apologize for that. I keep hearing, *Think about that when the time comes,* and, *You can't know how you're going to feel until it happens,* and it's driving me crazy."

"I can understand that," he said neutrally, while the doomed and dangerous words *birth plan* echoed in his head. In his experience, Fate took a perverse delight in throwing the best birth plans out the window from the moment labor began.

Better not tell her that.

Most definitely better not tell her that right now, when she was rubbing her lower back again and wincing as the pain tightened and then let go. "Braxton Hicks," she said knowledgeably. "I think it was the drive up. I should have taken a break to stretch."

She took a conscientious second helping of salad with no dressing. They talked about what a pretty drive it was, that last hour after you crossed from New York into Vermont. He offered her the fruit for dessert, and she ate this with the same attitude of confidence that she was doing the right thing. They talked about scenic attractions and prenatal yoga classes and where she might find a health-food store.

He offered her coffee to finish but she said no thank you, and by ten after eight she was pushing back her chair, running one hand over her belly and the other down the silky side of her outfit once again, and saying that she should go.

He leaped around the table to get the chair for her, but didn't quite make it in time. She was already on her feet and stepping away, her thumb tucking beneath the draping of her scarf to straighten it, while his hands came to rest uselessly against the chair back and his shoulder almost rammed the side of her head.

For some reason, they both froze.

No, not for *some* reason, for *the* reason.

The age-old reason.

The age-old thing that happened between a man and a woman.

The words for it were never right, never good enough. The clichés were like overwashed fabric, faded and weak. There was nothing weak about this. It was a slam in the gut, an overpowering onslaught against Andy's senses.

It had both of them in its grip for seconds he couldn't have counted even if he'd tried. Five? Forty? More? He saw the echo of his own awareness in her bright eyes, suddenly narrowed, and when he dropped his gaze to her full mouth, this didn't help, because her lips had parted and the light caught the sheen of moisture there and he could hear the breath coming in and out of her, too rapid and shallow.

She knew. She understood. She felt it.

I am not going to kiss you, Claudia Nelson. I am not going to pull that tight little knot down from the top of your head and run my fingers through your hair...

Nothing was going to happen between them, not tonight and not ever.

She must have reached the same decision. Her laugh was nervous and short. She reached up to twist a tendril of hair between her fingers. "Sorry, I really didn't expect you to get the chair."

"You looked tired, is all."

"I—I am. I'm sleeping so badly." She shrugged, smiled and frowned, all at the same time.

"Better get used to that."

"Not every baby is a bad sleeper. I've read up on strategies..."

"I'm sure you have," he drawled, trying not to smile.

She looked at him sharply, and there was a moment when the tension in the air could have switched. Awareness to argument. Sizzle to sniping. But they let go of both moods and she headed purposefully for the front door. "I'll take a bath. That seems to help."

"Might help soothe the baby, too, in a month or so."

"Yes, a lot of the books say that. Thanks for the meal, Dr. McKinley, I really appreciate it." *And I'm calling you Dr. McKinley so you'll forget what you saw in my eyes.*

He cleared his throat. "I'm right here, any time you need me."

"I'm fine. I'll take it easy tomorrow, settling in."

His last glimpse of her as she went along the porch to her front door was of her hand reaching around to her arched back once more, massaging it in a rhythmic circle just above the peachy curve of her backside with the flat of her fingers.

After this, they barely saw each other for several days.

Well, saw each other, but never for long at close hand.

She waved to him from the porch swing a couple of times as he was heading to or from work. He passed her in the street when he was jogging and she was walking back from the store, and they stopped for twenty seconds of greeting.

He heard her on her cell phone one morning, standing in the front yard to catch the best reception. "That was after the merger…Did you look under the original company name?…No, they're very similar." It sounded as if her office was having trouble letting go of her, or more likely the other way around.

One night, coming home after dark, he could see her front window lit up and there she was curled under a soft mohair blanket on the couch with a book in her hand. Even from this distance, he thought he could see a picture of a pregnant woman on the cover.

The weather warmed up a little, and he caught sight of her on Saturday afternoon, on a yoga mat in the garden, doing her pregnancy yoga exercises in a white ruched tank top and black stretch leggings, closing her eyes and breathing in, stretching her arms slowly upward, out and down, facing the beautiful sun, making a prayer position with her fingertips poised just below her chin.

That night, he was called out to assist in a delivery of triplets, and had about three hours' sleep.

On Sunday afternoon, she must have taken a nap—he'd tried, after his long night, but couldn't—because when he went into the garden himself, to put in a few hours of much needed work, a glance up at her bedroom window showed the blinds tightly closed.

When he'd raked the lawn clear of the last fall's leaves, tidied the shrubbery into shape and pruned the climbing roses along the side fence, he looked again and found the blinds open this time, to let in the late-afternoon light. He thought he could see a figure moving in there, but she was in the shadows, not near the window and the light. If she'd noticed him down here, it didn't seem as if she planned to come out and say hello.

Chapter Three

"Have an amazing time in Aruba, you two," Claudia told Kelly, on the phone.

She moved farther away from the window. Her landlord had just put down his pruning shears and looked in her direction, and she didn't want to have to wave and smile—or more truthfully, she didn't want him to know that she could see him so well from up here, and that she was looking.

He was wearing a pair of grass-stained khaki shorts, an ancient chambray shirt with the sleeves ripped off at the shoulder seam and some kind of boots, scuffed and clunky, with a scrunch of thick woolly sock appearing at the top. His bare legs were packed with knotty muscle and his dark hair had a twig and two leaves in it.

The sun shone on his uneven, sporty tan. His face and neck were nicely bronzed. His forearms were ropey and brown and dappled with sun-bleached golden hair.

His upper arms and those strong, knobby shoulders were paler, but they'd soon darken up if he kept to the gardening routine.

There was a ton of stuff to do out there. If he went on like this, Claudia would have plenty to look at between now and July.

Plenty of *plants,* she meant, of course.

"Oh, we will," Kelly enthused, to Claudia's half-listening ear. "And I'll be so relaxed as your birth partner next month, after our break, that the baby will just float into the world. I'm glad it's working out for you up there."

"It's working out great."

She ended the call, hoping Kelly hadn't caught the slight edge of doubt in her voice. It *was* working out great. She did her exercises every day, she read books on birth and baby care, she took naps and walks, she made nutritious meals, she played music to the baby, resting her hands on her belly to feel the movements change in response.

If it was too quiet and a little lonely and there wasn't quite enough to do—even on the days when she made or took three calls to or from the office—well, that was very temporary.

And if an old wooden Victorian with a big garden and creaky floors and a wraparound porch told you more than you wanted to know about the man in the other half of the house, well that was temporary, too. Once the baby was born, she'd be far too busy to pay any attention to Andy McKinley, in the garden or anywhere else.

She wouldn't care about his musical taste—everything from classical to country to driving rock, depending on his mood. She wouldn't notice the lack of a female voice and female footsteps, suggesting he was currently unattached. She wouldn't clock his hours or his clothing as he came and went—scrubs if he was headed to the hospital, neat professional attire for office-appointment hours, jeans and jackets and shorts and T-shirts for the various athletic things he apparently did in his free time.

One day, she had seen a canoe being strapped to the top of his pickup, and two men had arrived, bringing coolers, and they'd all gone off together in the pickup, wearing spray jackets and laughing a lot. She liked the way Andy laughed, and the way his arms moved when he was strapping the canoe in place.

She tried not to notice nearly this much about him, but how could she help it, when her days and her routine were so quiet? And when she was sleeping so badly, which meant that if Dr. McKinley was called out to an emergency in the early hours, she generally knew about this, too, because she heard the vehicle reversing down the drive.

Pull yourself together, Claudia. You're a mom-to-be, not a teenager pining for a date.

If only she was sleeping better!

Only another month…

The baby was coming. It was three in the morning, the early hours of Monday, but the delivery room at Mitchum Medical Center had an energy to it that Andy knew well.

Not long now. Almost there.

"Here's the head…take some short breaths now," he said. The shoulder was a little stuck. He needed a gloved hand and a well-practiced technique to free it, and then out came the slippery body. "Fabulous, it's a girl, Gina," he told the mom. "Congratulations, both of you." Nurse

Kate passed him a couple of instruments and he cut and clamped the cord.

The dad squeezed his wife's shoulders and buried his face in her hair. Both new parents were tearful and gushy, and there was no doubt about the health of the baby. She was crying and waving her little arms, but when they placed her on her mom's warm tummy she nestled and snuggled and it was wonderful.

But very late at night, second night in a row. His patients always seemed to give birth in clusters.

Andy delivered the placenta, checked the baby and the birth canal, made the necessary notes, all the small medical and administrative tasks that most new parents were too absorbed in their baby to notice. The high that everyone felt after a successful birth began to ebb and he started to think about a dark, quiet room, smooth sheets, closed eyes, warm dreams...

It was almost four when he turned into his driveway, and there was a light on in Claudia's front window. He saw a shadow moving behind the closed drapes as he came up the porch steps, and a floorboard creaked. What was she doing up this late? Was something wrong?

He was still thinking like a doctor who'd just delivered a baby. Didn't even pause to question his action, just knocked at her door and called out, "Claudia? Everything okay in there?"

He heard footsteps and the rattle of the doorknob. A gap of light appeared, partially blocked by a very tired and grumpy figure, holding a mug of hot chocolate with her little finger bent outward. "I'm pregnant and I can't sleep. Or breathe. What's *your* problem?"

"Called out for a delivery."

The gap opened wider. "Oh? At Mitchum Medical Center?"

"That's where all my patients go, unless it's something really serious."

"That's right, you told me that last week. I liked it when I took a tour, but haven't made a decision yet. Was it a good team? Did everything go well?"

"Textbook-perfect. Apart from happening in the middle of the night."

"Isn't that when they always happen?"

"Sure feels that way." He hid a yawn behind his closed hand.

"Come in. You look cold. I'm sorry I sounded snippy. If you have any ideas about the not-sleeping thing..."

He was in her living room before he knew it. She'd lit the fire in the brick-and-tile hearth and the warm air smelled of chocolate and a hint of woodsmoke. She was wearing a fluffy white robe and sheepskin boots. Free of makeup, her eyes had little creases at the corners from lack of sleep. Her hair sat in its usual knot, but it was lopsided and fuzzy with tangles. It looked like a robin's nest about to fall out of the fork of a tree.

"Looks like you're doing all the right things," he said. "Hot drink, warm air."

"Except I'm so hot in bed." She said it with total innocence, still grumpily focused on her discomfort and frowning at the fire, and he was shocked at the reply his very male mind came up with—luckily not out loud.

Hot in bed? I'll bet you are.

The grumpy expression and bird's-nest hair were weirdly sexy, for a start, as well as those fingers curved around her mug. And what was underneath the robe?

"It's so crazy," she went on. "In the daytime, I can go to sleep on the couch or on top of my comforter like that." She took a hand from the mug and snapped her fingers. "At night, when I climb between the sheets... not happening."

"So sleep on the couch at night."

"That's why I lit the fire. It's kind of soothing when it crackles. I can watch the flames till my eyes get sleepy. Right now, I think that's an hour away. Would you like some hot chocolate?"

She sounded wistful and eager at the same time, as if she really did want the company, and he wondered why this baby didn't have a father.

Why had there needed to be that crisp, distancing announcement, the day they first met, about sperm donation and planned pregnancy? Just how impossible was she to live with? Or just how exacting in her standards about men? Had something happened in the past to scare her off?

Or did she try too hard, like Laura?

Laura had crammed his house with heart-shaped objects and romantic sayings on fridge magnets. She'd told him, "I love you," so many times that the words lost all meaning. She'd created elaborate "date nights" after he'd worked eighteen hours straight and then sulked when he didn't want to take part, and generally poked and prodded at their relationship until it died like an overfed fish.

Claudia didn't seem exacting and impossible. Right now, she seemed adorable and sexy without knowing it and more alone than she should be a month from giving birth. He couldn't say no to her. He should say it, but—

"Hot chocolate would be great." He began to follow her to the kitchen, but she shook her head.

"Sit! I'm going to reheat this one while I'm there, I didn't give it long enough." She gestured to the mug in her hand.

He heard the refrigerator open and shut, and then the microwave. After a couple of minutes she reappeared, walking gracefully but super carefully with the two mugs so that the foamy chocolate didn't spill. She'd filled them too full.

The pink tip of her tongue appeared at the corner of her mouth, the way a little girl's did when she was working on a tricky drawing. Ms. Nelson would not have made a successful waitress if she had this much trouble balancing two drinks. Andy hid a smile, half amused, half captivated by the evidence of imperfection. He was beginning to realize that he couldn't think straight around this woman, and that there was a lot more to her than the efficiency and the plans.

They sat and sipped the chocolate. She asked him about his firewood supply. Would he mind if she lit the fire each night until the evenings were warmer? Or was that a nuisance, her using up the wood? Would he prefer her to use the furnace?

"The fire is fine," he told her. "I have one on my side, too, use it on snowy weekends mainly, when I'm planning to be home. There weren't enough of those weekends this past winter, so there's plenty left."

"I love the tiled surround. And the hardwood mantel." Her voice was lazy. She might not be able to sleep, but she'd lost the efficient edge he had heard in her daytime conversation.

It was so late.

So late, and he was beyond tired.

"They were boarded over when I first bought the house," he told her, feeling lazy about speech, as well. His voice creaked a little. "There was some hideous death-trap gas thing in this one. I took it out and took a sledgehammer to the boards. That was a great moment, when I saw the tiling and hearth all still intact behind the mess."

"Bet it was! I can imagine that hammer, too." She smiled, and he wasn't sure what she was thinking. "It was on my wish list, once, renovating an old house, but other things kept getting slotted in higher up."

"May still happen. You never know. Life takes curves."

He was getting sleepy. Really had been a long night. He'd only just gotten to sleep when the call had come from Gina Wilkins and her husband to say she was in active labor and they were heading to the hospital. Now it must be going on five.

He'd finished the chocolate. He put down the mug, but didn't want to jump straight up and leave.

"Curves," Claudia was saying. "It does."

They both thought about that for a moment.

A long, sleepy moment, with the flames dancing before their eyes—maybe if he just closed his for a second—and the room so...deliciously...warm...

And dark.

And downy, tucked under his chin.

Soft comforter, felt just like his. He decided fuzzily that he must be in bed...

He was definitely asleep. Deeply and righteously asleep, not just dozing as Claudia had thought at first.

Thinking about life's curves—like her parents' bitter, drawn-out divorce when she was ten—she'd heard the subtle change in his breathing and in the stillness between them. She'd sat beside him for several minutes, thinking that at any moment he would startle out of sleep and mumble an apology and she would usher him to the door so they could both get to bed. She was starting to feel as if sleep might be a possibility for herself, at last.

The pine log on the fire had begun to burn too low and the room wasn't so warm. Or maybe it was just because she'd been sitting so still, not sure whether to disturb Andy with her movement or leave him be. After a few more minutes, she'd eased herself off the couch, turned the lights low and gone to bring the spare comforter from the bed she had ready for Kelly.

She'd tucked it around her landlord—very important to remember, at that point, that he was her landlord—still expecting that the movement would waken him.

But no. She crouched uncomfortably beside the couch with her hand still on the puffy fabric she'd just spread across his body and studied his face and his breathing, and he was definitely still fast asleep.

Look at him, sighing into the comforter with the faintest of smiles on his face, the muscles around his jaw and eyes and cheeks so relaxed and smooth, his lashes all thick and dark on his cheeks!

He had freckles across that crooked nose.

She hadn't noticed them before. They were faint and light and sprinkled like gold dust on his skin, adding to the outdoorsy impression he gave. There was even a freckle on his top lip, right near the corner of his motionless mouth.

I want to kiss him.

I want to reach out and shape his face in my hands. I want to put my mouth on to his and take the heat of it until it wakes him up. I want him to reach for me, too, and pull me down, and make room for me on the couch with the whole length of him. And just keep me there. And kiss me. Hold me. Till morning.

I want the contact. It's been too long.

I want the connection.

I just want him.

A man.

Him.

It was her body talking, not her. Or it was her loneliness. Or her hormones. Or *something.* Something she had no control over. The thoughts didn't even come in words, they came in a surge of need that seemed more powerful because of all the extra blood in her body.

Think about that, Claudia.

Pregnant women had fifty percent more blood. It was one of the reasons she was so warm, most of the time.

You're pregnant, Claudia.

You have a baby due in a month.

The last thing you need is to feel like this.

About your landlord.

Your sexy, manly, capable, laid-back landlord.

She made a frustrated sound, and it seemed to make him stir. She was just about to whisper something to him about getting to bed—he could stay on the couch till morning, if he wanted, but she needed her room—when he reached out.

Was he still asleep?

His hand curved around the back of her head and pulled her closer. His eyes were still closed. His nose nudged forward. Where was the mouth he was looking for? Ahh...

His lips were so warm. She had to drag herself away. She had to! Or push him, or tell him, "Wake up, Andy. I'm not whoever you think I am."

But none of that happened. She let him kiss her, her own mouth motionless while his lips coaxed her. He mumbled, "Mmm," the sound coming from deep in his chest. He wanted a response. His dream self was growing frustrated that these soft lips beneath his weren't answering the kiss.

How could she answer it?

How could she *not*?

He tasted chocolatey-sweet and delicious and male and perfect. She hadn't been kissed for a year. She hadn't been *pleasurably* kissed for two, because the year-ago man had been a total disaster and had lasted just one date, and Claudia Nelson did not do second dates when the first one hadn't worked. It was inefficient, a waste of time.

She'd *never* been kissed like this, so slowly and dreamily and blindly.

She leaned deeper into the soft edge of the couch seat, and the only place to rest her arm was on his shoulder. She felt the baby move and settle, as if she…he?… felt at home inside her body, with all this give and relaxation. She felt a fullness deep inside her, an aching of muscles she hadn't known were there.

Oh, his mouth! How could it make such a connection with the rest of her body? How could she feel so full and yet so deeply throbbing with need? Her body had changed so much. She felt ripe down to her bones and to the tips of her newly filled breasts. She was a prisoner in her own skin—a prisoner who never wanted to leave.

She leaned in closer, parted her lips and touched him with her tongue then went deeper. Her body was boneless and helpless. He groaned. He stroked the back of her neck, ran his fingers up into her hair, found the knot on top of her head and suddenly the fingers went still.

Totally still.

But only for a moment.

"Claudia," he said, in a voice that was sleepy and gravelly and only very slightly surprised.

And then he went right on kissing her.

Chapter Four

Man.

You couldn't think in such a situation. It took Andy several seconds of groping thought, while his whole body clamored with one very simple feeling, even to realize where he was, what time it must be, what he was doing here.

Claudia. Hot chocolate. Middle of the night. Deep asleep.

He'd been dreaming. Not about Laura, or some fantasy woman, or anyone in particular. Just about femaleness and all the things a man loved. Silky hair and skin, sweet musky scent, softness and warmth, curves and weight beneath his hands, the touch of caressing fingers.

Man!

He was sure that it *was* a dream, that this delicious kissing feeling wasn't really happening, that it was all part of the cocoon of warmth that wrapped around him, the sense of peace and a good job done.

But when his dream hand reached up to run through dream hair that might have been blond or chestnut or black and he found that tight little bird's-nest knot with hairpins in it, his dream self had suddenly jolted into knowing that this wasn't a dream, after all.

This was Claudia.

But he still wasn't really awake...

Okay, so it was Claudia, sexy Claudia.

Wonderful.

She tasted delicious and she felt even better and she seemed as happy to stay in the dream as he was. He pulled her closer, found her peachy butt beneath his hand and levered her onto the couch beside him. There was just enough room.

They kissed long and deep and lazily. Her lips were like sun-ripened plums against his mouth. Sweet. Juicy. Warm. She burrowed against him like an animal needing warmth and contact, and she was so soft and relaxed.

Mmm, those breasts! Their fullness squished against his chest. The round bump below the breasts almost went unnoticed, the way she lay. Her robe had come apart and he could feel the graze of her big, hardened nipples. He wanted to touch them, cover them with his mouth.

But first the hair. Must do something about the hair. He found the cool metal bend of a pin and pulled, and the whole thing came apart and fell around his hand in a scented caress.

And then he thought, no, stop.

Because of the hair.

Because it felt so good like this, and yet this wasn't

the way she chose to wear it. She kept it scraped back
to signal her efficiency, or to convince herself that she
was in control. She was his pregnant tenant, choosing
single parenthood for he could only guess what reason.
Something had turned her off men. Or she'd been cru-
elly hurt. Or she was too rigid and controlling and competent for any man to stand.

None of those were good reasons for him to get involved like this, not a short-term fling, definitely not a
one-night stand, when a month from now there'd be a
baby in the picture.

"Claudia…"

She picked up on his changed intent just from the
way he said her name. Too fat and too clumsy, she
scrambled off the couch and made a pained sound as if
she'd hurt her back with the twisting movement.

"I'm sorry," he said quickly. Shoot, his vision still felt
heavy and fuzzy from sleep, and so did his brain. She'd
dimmed the lighting, and the fire was almost out. How
long had he been here? "I didn't mean for you to—"

"No, it's fine. I'm fine." She *had* hurt her back. She
was moving like an old woman, straightening with ex-
treme care and moving to grip the back of the adjacent
armchair. "It does this. It's the ligaments loosening, the
doctor said."

"I know. I'm sorry. I'm not apologizing for the back."
He swore. "That came out wrong. I am apologizing for
the back, and for—"

"No, it's fine," she said again. "I know what you're
saying. What you're apologizing for." He blinked and
focused and saw her flushed cheeks. "But it wasn't your
fault. I—I didn't wake you up when I could have. We
were both— This was a moment. Tired. Not thinking."

"Yes." He should have stopped there, but instead said, "It was nice."

Shoot!

"It was," she agreed, sounding thin. "But it's not what I'm looking for right now."

"No. Me, either…" *Stop, Andy!* "But it was really, really nice."

How many ways were there to *not* cross paths with the person who lived under your own roof?

Going out the side door in the mornings. Taking a peek from the window to make sure there were no stretchy, sexy, pregnancy yoga exercises taking place in the backyard. Listening for the sound of her car backing out of the driveway and checking which way it turned into the street—toward the store or away?

Claudia was as adept at the avoidance strategies as he was. Andy would see her climb off the porch swing as he arrived home after office hours or a stint at the hospital. One day, there was a note from her in his mailbox, saying that the bathroom faucet had begun to leak, and if he wanted to come change the washer, "any time Wednesday evening would be convenient," and she would leave her key under the mat, because she "wouldn't be at home."

He guessed she'd made deliberate plans to go out. Where? Dinner on her own? A movie, eating a carton of popcorn by herself in the cinema in the dark? It sounded lonely.

It wasn't his concern.

They were avoiding each other, and that was just what he wanted. Neither of them could afford to think about that long, breathtaking kiss during Monday's early hours, and neither wanted any risk whatsoever that it might be repeated.

They'd said to each other very clearly that it wouldn't be repeated, that it wasn't what either of them wanted, and, with his head, Andy knew this was true. They'd be crazy. It would be a disaster. And there was an unborn child involved.

But every now and then...

Man, it had been so good! It haunted his dreams.

His next serious sight of her came on a Thursday night just before bedtime ten days after her arrival, when the light from his bedroom window spilled out onto the wooden deck at the back of the house and showed her walking to and fro there dressed in a pair of loose cotton-knit chocolate-and-pink pajamas and what looked like a vintage pink silk robe.

He'd been just about to close the blinds when he'd caught movement from the corner of his eye and there she was.

Pacing.

Back and forth.

Lifting her face and pressing her lips together and whooshing out a breath.

Not happy.

Even from here, he could see her grimace and push down a sob.

Shoot! That wasn't just a twinge in her back, this time. She was in labor, and he could read her reaction from here. It wasn't in the plan, it shouldn't be happening yet. She wasn't due for another month. Things clearly *always* went to plan in Claudia Nelson World, and she was scared.

She was scared, she was on her own and he had no choice.

He left the blinds open, pulled on the casual athletic shoes he'd just kicked under the bed. Down on the deck, he found her still pacing. She'd gone farther, down the steps and into the yard. She had her back to him and he heard her whimper and groan as another contraction hit. It ebbed and she turned and saw him, and from her expression he felt as if he'd caught her out in something private.

Weakness, he realized. She didn't want to seem weak. She didn't want to give the naysayers—whomever they were—the slightest ammunition.

It was impressive and oddly troubling to see how quickly she composed herself. "I think I'm in labor."

"I know you are, Claud," he said quite tenderly, shortening her name as if he'd known her for years, instead of a tiny handful of meetings, a hot kiss in a waking dream, and a couple of waves and smiles. "Is it helping you to be outside? It's cold and you don't look that warmly dressed."

"I just needed some air. I thought if I walked around, the pains might stop, but they haven't." She smiled tightly. "You're right, it is cold." She gave a shiver and hugged herself. Her hair was down tonight, but drawn back with some kind of clip at the back of her head. She must have fastened the clip in a hurry because it wasn't straight, and it was slipping lower and lower through all that gleaming dark silk.

"Come in."

"I'll take another minute or two. The books say you should walk around."

"Let me get you a coat. The books don't say you should catch cold."

"I didn't bring a coat. Just a couple of jackets. It's April. Spring. I thought I'd just stay inside when it was cold out and the weather would be warm in a few weeks, by the time the baby was born. I didn't think I'd be outside at night."

"I can lend you something."

She nodded. "That would be great." She began to pace again, and he went inside and found a trench coat that his sister-in-law Alicia had left up here during the winter. Claudia would appreciate Alicia's expensive fashion tastes. The coat was by some designer. Alicia's clothes were always *by* someone, Andy had noted. He wasn't convinced that this was making model-gorgeous Alicia or his very driven orthopedic surgeon brother MJ happy, seven years into their marriage.

"I'm so sorry to disturb you like this," Claudia began, when he came back out, as if she'd appeared at his front door to borrow a cup of sugar.

"No problem," he answered, as if he had bags full of the sweet stuff.

She let him help her into the coat and he caught a tiny waft of her scent, like a tendril of flower-scented mist as she hugged it around herself. It reminded him far too vividly of the other night on her couch, his dream, the way he'd awoken and the way those moments lingered in his head.

She snuggled into the soft lining of the coat and instinctively adjusted the collar and pulled at the sides so that it sat the way it was meant to. Her hair bunched up, and the clip was caught somewhere beneath the coat fabric. She didn't even notice. If he'd been the father of her baby instead of her landlord who didn't want to get involved, he would have reached out and tucked the loose strands behind her ears, searched for the slipping clip.

"No problem," he repeated half under his breath,

while he fought and swiftly beat the resurging moment of male awareness.

What the hell was such a thing doing showing up now? Bad enough the other night. She was in labor, for crying out loud, so this was worse. They'd been right to keep their distance from each other, keep to the businesslike footing of tenant and landlord. But how could you do that when the landlord was a doctor and the tenant was ready to give birth?

"You must be about to go to bed and I'm sure you need your sleep," Claudia went on. The note of apology would have been more suited to an announcement that, most unfortunately, she was going to be a day or two late with the rent. "But if you could just give me some indication..." But then the politeness and frail pretense of efficiency fell away. "Help me! Could you? Dr. McKinley?"

"Call me Andy, for heck's sake," he growled, almost as helpless as she was.

She needed someone's touch. Warm loving arms, kisses of reassurance and murmured words about how great she was doing, but he had no right. And he didn't have rocks in his head. He'd got a grip about those.

"I don't know what to do. I just don't. This isn't supposed to be happening."

Okay, Andy, you're a doctor, you've been here hundreds of times before, and if this is a little different, just ignore it and go with what you know...

"Not very much to do at this stage." He kept his voice neutral and professional. "Everything's fine and under control, I promise. Keep walking around if it helps. We can go up and down the sidewalk, if you want." He took her arm and kept her pacing slowly, back and forth on the deck, while she took in his words.

"Out front? I'm not dressed—"

"You're dressed just fine. The birth is probably hours away. You probably even have time to get your labor partner up here, if she can leave the city within the next hour or two."

"She can't." Her voice rose and caught, and the distress she was fighting broke to the surface. "That's part of the problem. She and her husband Richie flew to the Caribbean a few days ago for a delayed honeymoon. That's why Kelly was so pleased when the crib arrived last week. She'd been afraid it might be delivered when they were—" She stopped suddenly. "The crib! I have nothing for a baby except for a car seat which I stopped to buy on my drive up! I have orders due. The swing. The breast pump. None of that has come yet."

"You have diapers," he couldn't help teasing. They would be too big for a month-early baby, but he wasn't going to tell her that.

"Just a handful of clothes. I don't even—ahhhh!" She stopped and gasped, bent with her hands resting on her knees, whooshed her breath.

Shoot, those contractions weren't that far apart! Ten minutes, if that.

He waited this one out with her, letting her grip his hands hard through the worst of it. She might not even have realized she was doing it. As it began to ebb, he asked her, "How long have you been having the pains?"

She took a couple of more breaths before she answered. "Since late this afternoon. I saw you arrive home from work. I was sitting on the porch swing. It was…uh…chilling down, so I went inside."

"Yes, I saw."

"The first one happened just after that. But the average active labor for a first-time mother is twelve hours."

He opened his mouth to give her a reality check on the word *average,* but she got in first. "I know it's highly variable. I do know that. But all the women at work seemed to be in labor for about a thousand hours—" Andy hid a laugh "—according to how they talked about it. Don't I have plenty of time? Time to have it stopped? It's too early."

"Only a month. The baby will be fine," he soothed her, because statistics said there was every chance it would be. Statistics sometimes lied, but he wasn't going to tell her that, either. She was anxious enough already, and beating herself up. "I doubt it can be stopped, though. Those are real contractions, aren't they?"

"Mmm-hmm."

"Ebbing?"

"Gone."

"Keep breathing. Keep walking."

"What did I do to make this happen? My yoga exercises—"

"—didn't bring on your labor."

"My birth plan—"

"—is obviously open to some tweaking at this point. But we'll deal with that."

"I'm all alone up here. Kelly can't be here. My parents... Well, my mom—" She broke off, and he understood that she didn't want her mom or her dad. "There's no one else I'd really want. I don't have anybody. I have nobody."

He could imagine his father groaning in the background about the getting-involved thing, but said it anyway, "Yes, you do, Claudia. You have me."

Chapter Five

"...So they were divorced when I was ten," Claudia finished. A floorboard creaked. She stood up from the couch, having only sat down a minute before. She was too restless to sit. They'd come in from the cold and were sitting in her living room, where the heating vents pumped out nice warm air. She hadn't lit the fire tonight, too distracted by the onset of the pains.

"Do you still see your dad?" Andy asked, then, "Is that another contraction?"

"No, not a contraction. Not yet. I just...can't sit, that's all."

"Helps to walk around."

"Yes... I did see him for a while, at first, after I went with my mom. Not lately. He's..."

Depressing. Downbeat. Useless.

She didn't say the words out loud. In any case, they were her mother's words, not hers, and they were usually uttered when there was expensive alcohol involved. She couldn't disagree. Her memories meshed with Mom's attitude. But still, something held her back from saying it. He was her father, after all.

Instead, she screeched to a mental halt and modified her language to something neutral and safe. "I can see why the marriage didn't last. I just wish it hadn't taken so long for them to sort out the divorce."

Sheesh, why was she telling Andy all this? She'd done so well in avoiding him since that night when her body had seemed like it belonged to someone else, and that kiss had felt like the best thing in the world.

The house was so quiet. The Vermont night was so quiet, the whole town of Radford fast asleep. She'd told him to go to bed. Really, there was no reason for him to be here. It was a terrible idea.

Her head said so, anyhow.

Her gut disagreed, once again her body wasn't hers, and Andy McKinley seemed to have the same opinion. "Let's stop talking about me going to bed," he'd said an hour ago. "I'm not doing that. I'm driving you to the hospital when it's time, and until then we'll talk or watch TV or whatever you want."

"Not TV." She didn't want her labor to unfold against a background of home shopping or ancient sitcom and crime-show re-runs.

"Nicer when it's quiet," he'd agreed.

Now it was one o'clock in the morning, they'd been talking and walking and even laughing a little, a couple of times, and the contractions were getting closer together. Eight minutes apart, then seven. Another one would hit at any moment. She paced, waiting.

"My parents are still together," Andy said. "Happy, I think. They fight, of course. Mom thinks Dad should slow down, maybe even retire, but he doesn't know how to do that. She thinks he puts too much pressure on my brother and sister."

"Where do you fit in?" He was only distracting her with conversation, she knew it, but she wanted to know about him, anyway.

"Middle child. Rebel and family diplomat at the same time, I'm told. My brother Michael's the eldest. We always call him MJ. Scarlett is the baby and the only girl, but that hasn't given her an easy ride."

"How did you end up here, when they're all in New York?"

"Needed to get out of the city. Liked it here."

"Why did you need to get out of the city?"

"Well, it can be a crazy place, can't it, New York? I still like the energy. I love to visit, especially in spring and fall…"

Suddenly, his dutiful effort at making distracting conversation stopped working, and she couldn't listen. His words faded into a background garble.

Okay, here it comes…

Hard, tight, agonizing squeeze, building higher and higher. She could feel it changing the shape of her belly. She felt as if her insides might be torn out. Andy cut off the pleasantries about New York and coached her through it, holding her hands while she squeezed and breathed.

At first, she'd been able to walk and talk through each one, but she couldn't, now. They were getting longer and more intense, as well as closer. "Five minutes," he said, at the contraction's height. "We might head to the hospital, I think."

"Which one?"

"You tell me. You were going to research—"

"I did. But make it Mitchum Medical Center," she gasped. "Stuff the research."

She'd thrown a few things into a bag a couple of hours ago and it stood ready by the door. She suddenly felt like a star actress catapulted onto the stage when she had no idea of what play she was in, let alone her cues and lines. She was the most important person in the scene, there was no way out, yet she was totally unprepared.

The cold and dark hit her as Andy opened the front door. He turned down the heating, turned off the lights, and the mundane actions gave a sense of finality. Claudia suddenly knew, in a moment of blinding insight, that she would be a completely different person the next time she came back to this house.

She'd only spent ten nights here, she barely knew the man beside her, even though they'd kissed, and her planned birth partner was two thousand miles away. The sense of plunging into the unknown nearly knocked her over, and then another contraction hit and she just had to ride it out, there on the front steps, with Andy's arms around her against the chill, and her head grinding into his big, hard shoulder as she tried not to moan and cry out.

He soothed her, reminded her to breathe, breathed with her, held her hands again. She couldn't let him go. She didn't know how she would have managed without him. Yet he was almost a stranger, and she wondered if she would even be able to picture what he looked like, this time next year when her as-yet-unborn baby hit its first birthday.

She didn't want to forget how Andy looked, and tried to fix his face and body language in her memory. He had that crooked nose and crooked smile, those dark, warm eyes, that lazy way of waving from the driver's seat of his car. He had hair that spilled onto his forehead when he hadn't brushed it in a while. He had a patchy tan and a strong grip and summer freckles. He had a mouth that felt like heaven, but she must not think about that.

Despite the short journey, another two contractions hit her as they drove, and there seemed no way to get comfortable, no way to ease the pain by her movement or her position. At the hospital, he roared into the ambulance entrance and leaped out of the vehicle, bringing a nurse and a wheelchair in less than a minute.

The nurse, Judy, clearly knew him. She was very reassuring and cheerful and warm, and Claudia felt immediately better in her company, until the woman said, "Thank you, Dr. McKinley, we can take it from here if you want to head home."

At which point kindly Judy became a fiend in human form, and Claudia, in the grip of her worst contraction yet, just wanted to yell and moan at her, *"No! Are you crazy? He can't leave! Do you have any idea?"*

"I'll need to park—can't stay in the ambulance bay—but then I'll be right back."

Judy looked at him in surprise. "Oh, you're staying, Doctor?"

"You can…go home…if you need to." Claudia made herself say it, forced the words out through the pain of the contraction with the last vestige of her pride and confidence, and then the pain built even more, the worst one yet, and she moaned, "No, you can't…you can't…"

"I'm not," he soothed her, his voice dropping low. "It's okay. Judy had the wrong idea. There's no way I'm leaving, I promise. I never intended to. Just need to deal with the car."

"Please…speed. Then run."

He laughed. For some insane reason, he seemed to think she was joking. "Good girl."

She moaned, "I am sooo not a good girl!"

When Andy came back from the doctors' parking lot at not quite a run but almost, Claudia had already been wheeled upstairs, and he had to wait for the elevator. It was only three floors. He thought about taking the stairs—felt an urgency to be back at her side that he'd seen in many a first-time father, and was somewhat astonished at finding in himself.

For hours at home she had clung to him, squeezed his hands with those soft, graceful fingers of hers. The crescents of her French-manicured nails had scraped at his skin in a way that was half pleasure, half pain. He'd talked to her, told her how great she was doing, all of that. He'd tidied her hair, taken the clip away. She hadn't even noticed.

They'd found out more about each other tonight, in those quiet hours in her half of the house, discovered a few things in common despite the yawning differences in the way they ran their lives. But did he really have any power to lessen the pain of the contractions with his presence?

When he reached the nurses' station, familiar with its smooth desk surfaces and trays of paperwork and harsh fluorescent lighting, he asked with too much urgency, "Where is she?"

"Delivery Room Two, Dr. McKinley."

"Thanks." He grabbed a disposable gown and cap and shoe covers, washed his hands at the corridor sink.

In the doorway of the delivery room, he heard May-Anne, one of the maternity floor's most experienced nurses, telling her, "There isn't time for an epidural, honey. I'd say you're almost there."

"But I need the bathroom. I need— Unh!"

"You're definitely almost there. Ah, good, here's Dr. McKinley."

"I'm not here to deliver. I'm here for the patient. She's a—" He stopped. *Tenant? Figure in my dreams?* "—a friend. Don't we have someone else?"

"Dr. Banks is on call."

"Then we're waiting for Dr. Banks. I'm here for Claudia," he repeated, grabbing a chair and scraping it toward the head of the bed.

Claudia was already gowned and she was sweating. "I'm not ready."

"You *are* ready, honey," May-Anne said.

The hospital wasn't. Not quite. Claudia fought through a contraction with her eyes closed and her breathing all over the place. Andy didn't know if she'd registered the special preemie crib being wheeled into the room, with its heated and humidified atmosphere, and its oxygen and monitors and equipment at the ready. There was every chance they wouldn't need it, so why was it here?

He threw a questioning look at May-Anne, who mouthed back to him, "Feels small for dates, heart rate slowing."

He nodded, while his gut dropped.

Dr. Banks appeared, snapping her gloves, her red hair covered by a tied disposable cap. There was a round of greetings and reassurances and questions. Claudia whimpered and moaned her replies, but insisted a couple of times, "I'm okay," then suddenly, "I need to push."

Andy felt strangely emotional, in a twilight kind of

state where this wasn't just a routine delivery and yet, apart from one misguided kiss, his personal involvement was so slight. He was such a last-minute, poor-quality substitute for the birthing partner she'd really wanted. Surely he couldn't be of much comfort.

And yet he wanted to be. He was so aware of that special equipment sitting ready.

"You're doing great," he told her. "Hold on to me. Push as hard as you want."

He sat behind her and she braced her shoulder blades against his arms, shuddering and groaning with the effort. He could smell her shampoo, a sweet, woodsy smell. May-Anne had dimmed the lighting to give the room more intimacy and warmth, and the low glow brought out all the different strands of color in Claudia's dark hair—copper and chestnut and ruby and sunshine.

"My hair," she gasped at the end of the contraction. "It's all over my face, I hate it."

May-Anne found a hair elastic and gave it to him and he had to take that sleek curtain in his hands, turn it into a rope and wind the elastic round it, low on her neck. His fingers brushed the soft skin and felt as clumsy as wooden clothespins, and the action seemed way too intimate, more intimate than a kiss, but she gasped out when he was done, "Thank you," as the pain built again.

If he'd been the baby's father, he would have leaned forward to kiss her during the short gaps between the relentless contractions, would have whispered private words of love and encouragement, instead of the cheerleading stuff he did as a doctor, which was all he knew. He said it again, "You're doing great," and it had to be enough.

Time passed. He wasn't sure how much. Maybe only ten minutes or so.

"We have a crowning head," coached Dr. Banks.

"One more push, honey," May-Anne said. Behind her, another nurse had the preemie crib ready, and Andy saw one of the local pediatricians, Dr. Grant Chung.

It took two pushes, but then the baby was out. Small. Messy.

"A boy! Claudia, you have a baby boy!" said Dr. Banks.

Claudia slumped back on the bed, momentarily exhausted, catching her breath. "A boy," she said, her voice filled with tears and wonder. "A boy!"

"We're going to just check him out before we give him to you."

"You'll be able to hold him very soon, honey."

He didn't look great, Andy saw as the baby was whisked away. Body too limp, face too blue. He couldn't see anything else before the baby disappeared behind a shield of professional bodies.

They had to work to get him to breathe and then he needed the oxygen, but they placed the tiny mask over his scrunched-up newborn face and his color and muscle tone must have improved fast because their voices lost the edge of urgency and Andy heard some crows and clucks of satisfaction, and the words "Pinking up, now" and "Look at that kick."

"It's okay," he whispered to Claudia. "Everything's okay."

"Where is he?"

"He's coming. You'll have him in a moment. You did great, Claudia."

"Oh, I want him, I want to see him."

"Here he comes."

She reached out her arms.

The baby was bundled in a warm nest of blanket with

the oxygen mask covering most of his little face. He wriggled and grimaced and Andy felt a wash of relief. He looked good. So much better. Healthy. Alert. He was going to be fine.

Claudia took him and cradled him against her breast. Her gown had slipped down and there was a pale swell of skin there, the perfect place for a baby's cheek. Her cheeks ran with tears and she was laughing and exclaiming, exhausted and euphoric and flooded with wonder, oblivious to any lingering mess and pain.

"He's perfect. He's beautiful. He's so tiny. Is—is he okay with the oxygen?" She turned to Andy, appeal and happiness and exhaustion all mixed up in her face, but May-Anne got in first with her reply.

"He won't need it for long, honey," she said. "Just because he didn't breathe on his own right away, that's all."

"He's perfect," Claudia repeated, turning back to her baby. "Ben. Benjamin James. Hi, Ben."

Andy fought to harden his heart against the desire to bend down and put his arms around the two of them as if they belonged to him. They didn't. Buttoned-up woman with her guard let down. Tiny scrunch-faced baby like an acorn ready to grow into an oak. They were not part of his life.

Perfect *now,* he told himself.

As perfect as even Claudia could want.

But how would things go tomorrow, and next week and the week after that? When she was so prickly and defensive, beneath her I'm-in-control exterior? When her expectations of herself and the baby were so high?

Chapter Six

"Mom?"

"Claudia? How are you, sweetheart?"

"Do you have a party there, or something? What's going on?"

"I just felt like some music. Is that a crime at four in the afternoon?"

"No, of course it's not a crime." The music was fine—clattery British rock from the sixties and seventies, played loud. Mom had been a fan of Clapton and Daltrey and the Stones for forty years. It was the slight slur in the voice that wasn't so fine. Four was a little early in the day for a society lady's champagne bottle to be open and almost gone, even if she was an ex-hippy. "Mom, you're a grandmother! I have a baby boy!"

"Hey... You weren't due for a month!"

"Ben had other ideas."

"Ben? Who the heck is Ben?"

"The baby."

"You're calling him Ben?"

"Benjamin James. Ben for short. Don't you like it?"

"Used to sound like a pet donkey's name to me, but I guess there are so many Bens around now, he'll fit right in."

Claudia bit her tongue. So her baby was a donkey, lost amongst the herd. Did Mom say things like this on purpose, or was she just train-wreck tactless when she'd been drinking?

"When was he born?"

"Early hours of yesterday morning. I've had a day and a half in the hospital—so busy with the routine!— but I'm going home within the next hour, so I wanted to call you first."

"So soon?"

"That's how it is, now, they don't keep you in long. But it's fine. I'm barely sore, I've slept, I just had a shower. I feel great, fantastic. I wanted to call before things get busy at home settling in. But I don't want you to feel you need to rush up. He's an angel, Mom, he's perfect. He barely cries."

"I'm not rushing up. Why you had to go to the wilds of Vermont, to some town no one's ever heard of…"

"I've explained why."

"I'll come once the weather is warmer, and once he's smiling. And of course he's an angel so far. They don't cry much the first few days. The nurses have it easy! You wait. Your aunt used to say the same thing to me every time with her four, when they were a couple of days old. Oh, he's an angel, he never cries. Like she'd personally turned down the volume on his lungs. And then whammy, three days later, they'd be screaming the roof off for hours at a stretch." She gave a hearty, smoke-filled, blurry laugh.

"Is that what I was like? I cried a lot?"

"You? You were hell for four months!" A harsher laugh, this time.

"And you still hold it against me."

"Of course I don't. You're a fabulous daughter and I don't deserve you." She tossed the praise out with ease, then went back to her previous theme. "I'm just warning you."

"I don't think crying is hereditary."

But Mick Jagger could get no satisfaction at that particular moment, and Mom hadn't heard. Claudia didn't repeat the words, just found a couple more pleasantries, which Mom echoed back to her with the same blurry warmth as before, and they ended the call. Claudia looked around the neat hospital room. What next?

Andy should be here at any moment. He'd insisted that it was no problem for him to take her home, of course he was taking her home, and she'd asked him to come at two. She was dressed and fresh. Her hospital bag was packed. Did she have time to make any more calls. Kelly? Or Dad?

No, not Dad. He wouldn't know how to react over the phone. She'd told him about the pregnancy in her Christmas card, but they hadn't spoken since. She didn't want to hear the wrong thing from another parent.

She would send a written announcement. She already had him on the list for that. Why change her mind? They were barely in contact. She hadn't seen him in years—four, was it?—and when they called each other, which only happened once in six months, if that, they were both so awkward about it. Dad always sounded as if her call had made him feel worse, and as if he hadn't been feeling great to begin with. Mom thought she shouldn't reach out to him at all and made fun of the cheap Christmas cards he sent.

And Kelly was probably on a beach.

So. No more calls.

The baby was still in his crib, fast asleep, wearing a hospital-provided sleepsuit in a preemie size, his going-home outfit she'd brought with her, to coordinate with her own clothes, all but forgotten, tucked back in her bag. It was miles too big for her son at the moment, as were all of the clothes she'd bought. That was another thing she'd have to organize once she was out of hospital.

Now, however, there was really nothing to do until Andy arrived but look at him, so Claudia did that.

Andy shouldn't have been so complacent about fitting the infant car carrier into his vehicle, it turned out. He'd had MJ and Alicia's kids in here a couple of times, but not until they'd graduated to a bigger contraption, which worked differently.

It took him a good ten minutes to nut out the correct way to buckle this one into the rear seat. He should have done it at home, but he'd already been running late, thanks to his appointments going overtime and spilling right through lunch, so he'd just grabbed it from the trunk of Claudia's car, thrown it in and made the drive, as if the postponed task would somehow go quicker here in the hospital parking lot.

It didn't.

He'd agreed to Claudia's requested two o'clock, and he knew she would be waiting. It was already twenty after two, and in her eyes the baby's future admission to Harvard was probably in jeopardy now that Andy had destroyed the schedule. Like a panicky first-time father, he almost ran through the lot, but then he took a hospital back-entrance shortcut like a seasoned member of staff.

It was an odd mix. He wasn't comfortable about it.

And then he reached the doorway of Claudia's room.

She was sitting on the edge of the bed, leaning over the crib, transfixed by the sight of her baby sleeping. He was a funny, tiny little munchkin. He'd only weighed four pounds, two ounces, and coming early meant he still had the downy hair on his body that full-term newborns had usually lost, as well as a black cap of it on his head that looked like a bad toupee. He was red and scrawny, and flat-faced from his journey through the birth canal, and nobody, but *nobody,* could have called him beautiful.

Nobody except his mom.

She heard Andy enter the room and she looked up, and he saw the glow in her face and the maternal softness in her body. She'd dressed for this moment, he realized, in a pretty patterned top with a round, scoopy neck and matching leggings. He'd seen this new-mom look so many times—the full breasts, the soft tummy, the stretchy clothing, but it seemed different this time. Sexy and fresh in a way he had no right to notice.

She had her hair twisted on top of her head as always—although maybe it wasn't quite so tight and neat—and she wore delicate gold earrings and a brush of makeup. Even her neatly packed bag coordinated with the whole effect.

She looked textbook-prepared and relaxed, and above all just *happy.*

He cleared his throat. "Sorry I'm late."

"Oh…it's fine. Just a few minutes. He's sleeping.

The nurse said just to call her when we're ready for the wheelchair." It was hospital policy that new moms left the building comfortably seated, with their baby safely on their lap.

"And are we ready?"

"Oh...yes. He's due for a feed at three o'clock." She touched the side of her breast unconsciously. "We should be home and settled in by then."

"It's almost two-thirty."

She frowned. "That late? Then it's going to be tight."

Her gaze went back to her baby as if pulled by a string. She smiled, captivated, and let go of the scheduling anxiety. With one-on-one tutoring, little Ben might still make Harvard after all, despite the snafu.

"Good news, though," Andy told her. "The bassinet you ordered arrived this morning."

"That'll just be for naps, once Kelly brings up the portable crib," she informed him.

"And our office staff put together a couple of more things for you—a bath, some linen and some preemie clothes."

"Oh, wow! Oh, that's wonderful of them, when they don't even know me! Please tell them thank you, until I have a chance to send a card. I'll be able to give it all back, as soon as the rest of my internet orders arrive."

"No need, they say. You've saved them a garage sale."

She laughed. "Tell them they're the ones who've saved me."

Andy summoned the nurse and the wheelchair. Claudia settled herself in and reached for her precious bundle. Snuggled into her arms, baby Ben gave a huge yawn in his sleep, then went still and peaceful again. "I can't believe he didn't wake up," she murmured. "He's such a good baby." Andy had to smile at the mix of smugness and wonder in her voice.

All the way along the corridor, down in the elevator and out through the lobby, everyone who passed them smiled, and several said, "Congratulations!" Claudia beamed at them and rightly took it as her due.

Andy...

Felt like a fraud.

Was a fraud.

This wasn't his baby. This glowing, beautiful mother was his tenant, not his wife.

But what could you do? Wear a sign? *I'm the land-lord. It's not my fault. I just happened to be there.* Nobody wanted a lengthy explanation. He just had to accept the warm bath of well-wishing. Seemed as if the whole world was happy to see a couple with a new baby.

"I am so grateful for this," Claudia said when he'd unbuckled the car seat and brought the still-sleeping baby inside the house, then returned to the vehicle and carried in her hospital bag.

"What else?"

"Nothing. You've been amazing. But I won't need to trouble you anymore now. It's all under control."

"If you're sure..."

"Really. They helped me establish his routine in the hospital. I'll feed him and change him, then organize a few more things while he's sleeping. He should be down for three hours." She seemed to be parroting a memo-rized schedule. "I'll wake him if he hasn't wakened by six o'clock on his own, to keep our timetable on track." She gave a happy, confident smile, her cheeks pink and pretty. "Please, don't worry. I'm fine."

So Andy headed back to his office for an afternoon of minor procedures on his patients, his brief episode of fatherhood under false pretenses already a thing of the past—at least as far as Claudia was concerned.

He didn't know whether to be enormously impressed or to laugh out loud.

Neither, he discovered ten days later.

You couldn't laugh.

Not when she looked like this.

She answered his knock at her door wearing her pajamas at six in the evening. Her hair looked as if she'd been dragged backward through a bush. She had a cloth diaper on one shoulder, covered in what looked like—but wasn't—cottage cheese. She had the baby on her other shoulder, and his looks hadn't improved over the past ten days.

Or maybe that was down to the screaming. High-pitched and shuddery and relentless and *loud.* His face was red and screwed-up and frantic. In Andy's experience, only a healthy baby could cry that way, but a first-time mom wasn't always up with this piece of wisdom.

She burst into tears. "I am so sorry...to be... disturbing you like this. Through the *walls!*" She stood aside for him to come in, and he stepped forward, with a creepy feeling at the back of his neck, as if his father was standing there on the porch steps behind him, arms folded across his chest, mouth pressed into a tight line.

Andy, you are getting involved. Back off right now!

As if getting involved was like playing with mercury or TNT.

"That's not why I'm here," he said.

"But you can hear him next door." It was a statement, not a question. Of course Andy could hear him next door. She bounced the baby and went "sh-shh" a few times, but little Ben was crying too hard to care.

"I think they can hear him in Canada."

Nope, not funny, apparently.

"No, but it's not disturbing me," he went on quickly. "Just wanted to check how you're doing. He was crying this morning when I left for work, I think."

I know.

Because the crying had already lasted at least an hour at that point.

She paced toward the kitchen and he followed her, but then she turned and headed off in a different direction, and he ended up just standing there watching while the words streamed out of her and she hid her tearstained face beneath her hair. "I don't know what's gone wrong. We were doing fine, I did what the books said, and then a week ago he was a little fussy, and the next day he was worse, and since then worse still, and I think it's because his routine is disrupted, but he's the one disrupting it and I don't know how to get him back on schedule."

"Routine is a pretty fragile, flexible thing with newborns."

Inadequate, Andy.

"I'm supposed to let him cry it out, but I can't. He's distressed. He's not doing it on purpose. I'm supposed to keep him awake if it's not time for his nap, but what happens if I've only just got him to sleep from when he didn't have the previous nap?"

"Well, I think—"

"He's only eleven days old. Is it because he was early? He's too young for the same routine as a full-term baby? Kelly is coming up tomorrow—I love her, she's only just back from Aruba—but how can I have her here, when we're like this?"

"I'm sure she'll—"

"The only thing that seems to comfort him is feeding. He's on my breast for hours, sleeping and waking, but the books say I have to keep it to strict times. I'm trying to use the breast pump in between, but that's harder than I thought it would be."

"If you want, our practice nurse could give you—"

"The books say I'm supposed to be getting all of that onto a schedule so he's familiar with a bottle and expressed milk for when I go back to work..."

Andy finally seized on the bit about Kelly coming up, instead of doing what he wanted to, which was finding "the books" and throwing them across the room. "It's great your friend will be here," he cut in firmly. "How long is she staying?"

"Four nights."

Only four?

Not enough.

"Just enjoy each other's company. Forget about the routine while she's here. If it comforts him to be on the breast, then keep him there. You can hold off on mastering the pump for a little longer. But as I was saying, our practice nurse Maggie could give you some help in that area, if you want."

Inadequate. Inadequate.

And yet, still, *involved*.

"What's Kelly going to think? I feel like such a failure. And the books say it's because I *am* a failure. Because I'm not being strict enough about the timing. Because I'm losing heart after the first rough patch, when I should stay strong. I have to push through this. But how can I push through it when he's hurting and I'm dying from lack of sleep?"

He didn't know what to say. He was definitely going after those books, vigilante-style.

She seized on his helpless silence and began another round of apologies, backed him toward the door and sent him home. "Thank you, Andy, thank you so much for everything, I'm so sorry to disturb you, I'm fine, really." And when he reached the—comparative—silence of his own half of the house, he found he was sweating and wretched.

Involved, but not. Caring, with no reason. Powerless to really help.

The baby was still crying.

Should he have not gone to Claudia in the first place? Should he have forced her to let him stay? What could he have done to help? Babysitting?

He wasn't the father. He'd been at the birth, but he and Claudia were nothing to each other. They didn't fit with each other's plans. The best kiss in the world couldn't change that. He felt angry at her and at himself.

At her for falling into the classic stereotype of the professional woman who thinks motherhood will be a breeze, given her corporate efficiency and organizational skills, and goes to pieces the moment she finds she's wrong.

At himself for caring, for hearing the crying next door and wanting to help instead of swearing and turning his music louder, for feeling bad when he didn't have the answers on tap, for feeling selfishly as if he himself had lost something precious, because she was no longer that pretty, perfectly dressed, proud, in-control, beaming new mother with a peaceful little bundle that she'd been ten days ago.

For kissing her and muddying the already confused waters of their non-relationship.

"Dad is right," he muttered. "She wanted to do this

on her own. She's my tenant. She has her friend coming up. I'll talk to Maggie about a home visit. Other than that, I am not getting involved."

Chapter Seven

"So, tell me about him." Kelly snuggled deeper into the couch and fixed an inviting expression on her face. She wanted girl talk. Her third night in the house, and they'd managed so little of it.

It was nine o'clock. Claudia had just put Ben into his bassinet, and—hold your breath—so far he'd stayed asleep. She had the baby monitor on the coffee table and it wasn't making a sound. She'd become so dependent on that monitor! How had people managed before they were invented?

"You mean my landlord?" she answered her friend.

"I mean the man who took my job, being with you at the birth. You must have wanted him there, or you would have asked him to leave."

"I—I— Yes, I did want him, I guess. But I probably would have appreciated the involvement of Attila the Hun, at that point."

"Oh, garbage!"

"No, seriously."

"No, *you* seriously. Think about it. Be honest. Would you have wanted your boss there? Or the guy from the convenience store who's always trying to hit on you? Or even that waiter we both thought was cute that night at Richie's birthday dinner?"

"Okay...no. None of them."

"So tell me about your landlord. It has to be more than just wanting someone's hand to dig into with your nails when you were in pain."

Claudia snuggled into the couch, too. Kelly had made them each a mug of hot chamomile tea. The gentle herb was supposed to find its way into her breast milk and soothe the baby. Kelly was being such a great friend, but Claudia was so tired.

Girl talk. How did you do that, again? She'd forgotten. She couldn't remember the point, or why it was fun. She and Kelly had spent years on girl talk, verbally pulling their dates apart, fixing each other up with promising men and then extracting a full report, over coffee or lunch, or in side-by-side chairs at the salon.

He has a five-room East River condo, it turns out, but no sense of humor.

I heard some great gossip about celebrities—he did the casting for the movie that won the Best Editing Oscar last year, I've forgotten its name—but, sheesh, did he ever think he was God's gift to women!

And then Kelly had met Richie and hadn't said a word about him until they were almost engaged, and Claudia had been...okay, hurt...but, now, suddenly, she understood that there were some things you didn't want to talk about too much, or talk about in the wrong way.

She didn't want to talk about Andy McKinley in the wrong way, she wanted to protect...

What? Was it the fact that they'd kissed? It had been crazy, that. Hormones or loneliness or gratitude. She had a child, now. Everything was different. No more bad dates. No more *good* dates. No dates at all, for a long time, until she'd built her maternal bond and found her parenting feet and, damn it, *had some decent sleep!*

"Well, because he's a doctor, I think," she finally said, trying to be honest to Kelly, and to herself—honest and, even more important, rational and sensible and in control—about why she'd found Andy's presence so necessary and right that night. It wasn't simply that she'd had no choice because there was no one else. "He's been through it so many times. I knew he wouldn't panic or faint or make it all about him, or expect anything in return."

"Like sex?"

"Like sex."

"He's cute."

Lordy, he's more than cute, honey...

Claudia's lips went prim. "You've just gotten back from your honeymoon, Kel, are you supposed to notice other men?"

"I can make an objective assessment. *You've* just had a baby, you probably think you'll never want sex again. How long do they say? Six weeks?"

"They've softened on that. When you feel like it, they say."

"Who's they?"

"The books. The nurses."

"So, do you ever want sex again? I'm asking because Richie is a little daunted by the idea that I might never want sex again once we have kids."

"I'm not a huge authority, Kelly, I haven't actually had sex for quite a while, if you remember."

"So my objective assessment of your landlord's cuteness is worth more than your hormone-addled aversion."

"I thought we were talking about Richie's concerns."

"We're talking about anything we want. Men, sex, birth."

The baby monitor decided to enter the conversation. *"Wahh..."* it went.

Why did she feel like this? It was the last sound in the world that Claudia wanted to hear. Her heart sank. Her bones ached in exhaustion. And yet she couldn't ignore it, she couldn't harden that sinking heart. Ben was crying for a *reason,* and that reason wasn't to torment her. He was only two weeks old, he didn't think that way, and she loved him so much.

"Maybe he'll settle," Kelly said.

"I'll wait a little," she agreed, but every minute of it felt like an hour, and after five minutes he hadn't settled, his cry had just grown higher and louder and more frantic and she felt as if she'd tortured him by waiting. "I can't," she told her friend.

"No, of course you can't. Go, then."

She brought the baby down to the couch. He was hungry again. She could tell by the way he rooted for her breast when he smelled the milk. His little bud of a mouth didn't latch on properly and she felt a piercing stab of pain in her sandpaper-sore nipples. They were so dark and big, they seemed like they belonged to someone else, but boy, when the baby's mouth got hold of them the wrong way, she knew they were hers!

With a finger, she broke the suction, rolled his lower lip down and tried again. Still painful, but he had a deeper grasp and would get more milk this way, with less soreness for her and less effort in sucking for him. He tired himself out with it, she suspected, and he fell asleep before he'd filled himself up.

Kelly watched. "You're amazing, Claudia."

"Hah!"

"No, you are. Doing this on your own."

"I didn't do it to be amazing, I did it because I wanted a child and it didn't look as if it was going to happen any other way, and I was running out of time, and I wasn't going to get bitter, I was going to take control."

"Sorry to harp on about this but...your landlord. Is he single?"

"I haven't asked."

"You might have noticed, though."

"I haven't seen any women coming and going," she admitted reluctantly.

"So...?"

"Don't."

"He had a head start, didn't he, being at the birth?"

"Please, don't!"

"Okay, okay, the timing is wrong."

"The timing couldn't be more wrong, and I am not messing this up by suddenly getting desperate to find a father for the child I chose to have on my own. I'm not going to go for any port in a storm, Kelly, I'm just not!"

"No, I get that. You're right. You always have everything so well worked out, and so under control."

"Except my baby crying."

"Except that."

The friend, Kelly, didn't stay long enough, and wasn't enough of a help, Andy concluded from his non-involved position on the outside of the whole situation.

Not that he blamed Kelly. He guessed that she was trying.

One morning, just before heading for work, he saw her set out with the baby in a stroller, both of them well protected against the morning chill. He could see she was trying to give Claudia a break, but Kelly must only have gone a block or two with the stroller when Claudia herself came rushing out of the house, just as Andy was reversing down his driveway.

He lowered the window and met her frantic face. "What's up?"

"Kelly took Ben for a walk, but she forgot the baby wipes."

"The wipes are that urgent?"

"They might be. You have no idea. There's *force* down there, sometimes. In all directions."

"Need a lift?"

"Are you headed for work?"

"Yep."

"Then I'll say no to the lift. They went in the other direction. But thanks."

"It's fine. We can deliver the wipes and then I'll drop you back home."

"Oh, would you? That'd be great."

She sat beside him as if the wipes were an urgent blood delivery, and when they caught up to Kelly, she jumped out of the car and told Andy, "Don't wait. I'll walk along with them."

Kelly looked a little bemused by the whole thing. "You were supposed to be resting," Andy heard her say.

"I'm fine. Sometime he can need those wipes pretty urgently. Don't make me give you details. And plus, I got a little nervous about the stroller brake. You have to make sure it goes on right, or you'll think it's on when it's really not and the stroller might roll. I forgot to tell you."

Andy turned the car around. In his rearview mirror, just before he drove away, he saw Claudia bending beneath the stroller canopy to tuck the blankets around Ben's chin exactly right.

The next afternoon, Kelly left, and Andy couldn't know for sure, thanks to his days spent out of the house, but he suspected that Claudia hadn't let her friend take care of the baby for more than three minutes at a stretch.

He said to Maggie at the office, "Can you schedule a home visit to my tenant? She has a breast pump she can't figure out."

There. That wasn't involved. It was professional.

He didn't even ask Maggie for a report on how the home visit went.

Andy would never know what it cost Claudia to make and deliver to him this pecan pie, she swore.

He must not be allowed to guess how many days it had been in the planning stage, after Kelly left—all too soon! How many times the trip to the store for the ingredients had been postponed, on the scheduled day of her weekly shopping trip, because Ben needed a diaper change, or a nap, or a feed, or a diaper change, outfit change, nap *and* feed, all at the same time.

He must not get an inkling of how she'd rushed to make the pastry while Ben slept, left the filling half finished when he cried, almost burned the pattern of nuts that formed the decorative topping because she'd fallen asleep with the baby on her lap on the couch when he finally settled. He must not discover how long it had taken her to shower and dress so that she presented a semblance of her former self when she brought the pie to his door.

Come hell or high water, he was getting this thing.

She owed him.

Effusive gratitude for all he'd done, plus a heartfelt apology for the harridan who had greeted him at the door just a week and a half ago, sobbed at him in hysterical distress and then yelled his head off.

She was doing much better now, and she wanted him to know it. She'd discovered that you could actually learn to live without sleep and "me" time and uninterrupted showering, and soon Ben would have to get himself onto the routine and it would be okay. The visit from Maggie the practice nurse had been great, and the breast-pumping thing was starting to work, so there was genuine progress.

She hadn't tried to find a gesture of thanks for him while Kelly was here. She really, really did not want her friend getting any more ideas on the subject of the cute, convenient landlord. But now the thanks were overdue, and this was a kind of send-off, also, a signal that she didn't expect anything more from him.

They'd kissed. They'd acknowledged the mistake. He'd been at the birth and he'd brought her and Ben home, and now her life had totally changed, and not in quite the way the books said it would.

Which meant they were done.

Balancing the pie on the flat of her hand, while her foot bounced the stroller in the soothing rhythm that sometimes—only sometimes—settled the baby, she rang Andy's doorbell.

The door opened, and she chirped an insanely upbeat, "Hi!" that said, *it wasn't me, last week, that woman with the tangled hair and stained pajamas.*

"Hi." Cautious. He noticed the pie, which she would have been actively shoving in his direction if she'd moved another inch. "Hey, you didn't have to."

"No, I know, but… Well, yes, I did. Or you might have cut short my lease."

He laughed, which felt nice. "Come in."

"No…"

"Come in! You've brought the baby, put him in the stroller specially—"

"Well, no, he was already in the stroller. It's the only thing that seems to work." It was Ben's birthday today—he was three whole weeks old.

"But it is working?"

"He's been taking milk from a bottle pretty well the past few days, too. I even have a little frozen now. I think if I can just keep going another few weeks, we'll be onto the routine and everything will be fine." How many times had she said this to herself? A thousand? It sounded different, out loud. Less convincing. More desperate and neurotic.

"Uh… Have you thought that maybe everything could be fine without the routine?"

"What do you mean?" She bumped the stroller wheels gently across the threshold and held her breath. *Don't wake up, little man. Oh, but you're beautiful, I can't stop looking at you!*

"That maybe it's your tension about the routine that's contributing to him being unsettled."

"Babies are more contented if they have a routine." The books said so. And the books made sense. She'd read so many of them, taken so many notes on their methods. So how could they be wrong?

"Well, yeah, broadly I think that's often true, but not always," he said, heading for the glassed-in porch at the back of the house. Claudia envied him the porch. She didn't have a glassed-in part in her half, because the house wasn't symmetrical that way.

"Broadly? Not always?" Ben began to stir and make sounds. He *couldn't* be waking up already! She rocked the stroller back and forth.

"Younger babies in big families manage a disrupted schedule. They can be very contented, because everything is so relaxed. The mom is experienced and doesn't stress. If she has to hold her baby, she holds him on her hip or her back or her chest. If he settles, she puts him down. The baby soon sleeps through the noise of a busy household."

"You're saying my routine for Ben is too quiet?" *Don't wake up, Ben, feel me rocking this thing. Rock-a-bye baby, on the treetop...*

"I'm saying there aren't as many hard and fast rules as you're trying to put in place."

I'm not singing lullabies in front of Andy. They never work, anyhow, unless I'm holding the baby. Oh, Ben... Oh, baby...

He wasn't going to settle. She knew the signs by now. It wasn't simple hunger, this time. Something was bothering him. Beneath the fuzzy blanket in the stroller, he drew up his little legs and let out a piercing wail of distress, which she felt deep in her heart.

She was supposed to leave him to cry, so that he learned to settle on his own. It made so much sense on paper. Even after that night with the baby monitor, Kelly had tried to help her follow the rules, but Kelly had been horrified by how much the baby cried and how little the rules helped.

By the end of her friend's visit, Claudia was afraid she'd put back Kelly's own pregnancy plans by at least two years. Kelly had offered to take the baby for another walk, after the first fiasco when Claudia had forgotten about the wipes and the brake, but it didn't seem like a good idea. Kelly would have felt so bad if she'd done something wrong and the baby had cried.

"I can't do this," Claudia muttered. Out loud, with a tight smile. "Sorry, Andy." She picked up her baby. Oh, he was so sweet, he smelled like cheesecake. On her shoulder, while she moved her hips in a rhythmic figure eight and gently thumped his back, his crying began to ease, but she knew what would happen if she tried to put him down again. "Let me head back next door. You have the pie safely. If you could just wheel the stroller for me?"

"Stay."

"How can I?"

"Give him to me."

"It won't work." But she handed the little bundle over, too embarrassed to make a big deal of it.

Andy looked so good with him, as if he'd done this before, and not just as a doctor. He had the right gentle sway, the right big curved hand beneath the little padded butt, the right soft grin on his face, dropping into a sober expression when he crooned in a low voice, "Hanging in there? Feeling better now?" Ben looked so tiny against his shoulder, the fuzzy little head gently touching the square, slightly beard-shadowed jaw.

He *had* done it before, it soon turned out. "I have a niece and a nephew," he explained. "Not to mention all my ob-gyn patients."

But he couldn't settle Ben enough to put him down, and Claudia's hands itched to snatch the baby back. He looked tiny on that big male shoulder, like a little blue frog in a stretchy suit. He wriggled and bobbed his head against the back of Andy's supporting hand, and the moment they thought he was soothed enough and went to lay him back in the stroller, the crying picked up again.

Claudia took him back and paced around Andy's house. "You were going to cook," she said, seeing the jar of pasta sauce on the kitchen counter.

"I'm bailing on that, getting take-out Chinese. Want some?"

He was doing it because of her and the baby, she knew. If she had any amount of determination, she'd take Ben home and let Andy get on with his life, but, oh, she was hungry and she had no plans for a meal, just a few vague possibilities based on what she'd tossed into her cart at the store, even though the books said you should sit down and plan all your meals at least a week in advance, and—

"That sounds great," she told him weakly.

If Mom could see me now...

Her mother had said she would come up when the baby was smiling. Babies smiled at around six weeks. Another three weeks to go. It would be the end of May, by then, which surely had to count as warm enough for her mother, even in Vermont.

If I call her tonight, after I've had a good meal and settled the baby, and get some exact dates from her, then I'll have something to look forward to...

"Anything special you like?" Andy asked.

"Whatever comes. Carbs." The breast-feeding seemed to make her starving the whole time.

He picked up the phone and she heard him reel off a lengthy order of fried rice and General Tso's chicken and mu-shu pancakes and Singapore noodles, far too much for two people. "You're going to make me take home the leftovers for tomorrow, aren't you?"

"Yep. Going to argue?"

"No…"

He went by car to collect their meal. "I know this place. Home delivery is slow."

It felt strange to be alone in his half of the house. Claudia found the diaper bag hanging over the back of the stroller and changed the baby on the floor, then spread a quilt there and let him have a kick before she put a new diaper on. The books said that a kick helped sometimes.

He seemed to enjoy it. His little legs moved as if he was riding a bicycle, but then he grew fretful again and she worried that he might be getting cold, so she taped the fresh diaper in place, pushed his legs back into their stretchy suit—oh, she'd been so awkward about dressing him at first, because she felt he might break if she pushed the wrong way, but this at least was getting better—and wrapped him in a flannel blanket and offered him her breast.

"There, little man, is this what you want?"

Seemed to be.

They sat there. The couch was squishy and deep and the baby warm in her arms. She loved when he looked contented like this, in a rapture of feeding and sleep. She couldn't believe that feeding him felt so natural and right, now that the soreness was subsiding and her milk seemed plentiful and flowing.

There was the sound of an engine in the driveway and the front door clicked and Andy was back, accompanied by an aroma that made her stomach growl. Ben was still feeding.

He's a doctor. He's seen it before.

But still it felt way too intimate, the dark head snuggled against her darkened nipple, her breast all full and taut, and most of it on view. Should she stop?

Andy didn't seem to think so. "I can set it out here, if you can eat with one hand." He didn't stare, and he didn't look away.

"If I couldn't, I would have starved by now, " she retorted. She used to eat with one hand at her desk, too, going through budgets and spreadsheets and reports. She could eat with one hand, but not while Ben was eating, too. Andy disappeared into the kitchen and she used the opportunity to ease the baby from her breast, fasten her nursing bra and smooth down her top. It hadn't been a long enough feed, but for now her little man seemed content.

From the kitchen, Andy brought bowls and forks and serving spoons, opened the containers and set out paper napkins. "Can I fill your bowl?"

"Yes, please." She sat the baby on her knee facing the coffee table, and curved her arm around him so he was balanced and supported, even though he was still way too young to really sit. He didn't seem to mind. As she'd indicated to Andy, they'd done this before.

There was a flat-screen TV in the corner of the room, not so big that it suggested an obsession with sport, but a good size for the room. Andy caught her looking at it and asked, "Want to watch something? A movie?"

"CNN?" She realized out loud. "I haven't switched on a TV since I came home from the hospital." She'd listened to New Age music when Ben was supposed to be sleeping, in the hope that it would soothe the baby, and classical music when he was awake, to stimulate the development of his brain. "I have no idea what's happening in the world."

Suddenly this didn't seem like a good thing. She was going back to work in just over three months, she needed to know about the markets and the world events that made them rise and fall. The world didn't end at her doorstep just because she was a mom, and determined to be the best, most organized mom on the planet.

"CNN, sure." Andy pressed some buttons on the remote, and there was the finance news she'd wanted, all the names she knew. Nasdaq and Nikkei and Dow.

They brought a sense of well-being, and she realized she'd missed the market dips and surges the way she missed Kelly. She and the markets were friends. She was familiar with them. She enjoyed their company.

Why was Andy looking at her like that?

"What?" She frowned at him.

"Nothing..."

She kept frowning.

"I liked the look on your face just now, that's all."

"Well, I enjoy this stuff."

"No need to apologize." He was still trying to hide a smile.

Actually, she liked the look on *his* face, too, even if he was laughing at her. Better not keep looking...

"You'll have to give me stock-market tips," he said.

"Don't go with your gut," she answered automatically, watching her baby, her food and the screen. The Nasdaq had dropped.

"No?"

"Everybody thinks they have great gut instincts when it comes to the market. Trust me, unless they're Warren Buffet or someone, they don't. And he doesn't have a gut, he has a brain and a lifetime of using it. Even he probably thinks it's his gut by now, but it isn't." The Dow had dropped, too.

"You have strong feelings on the subject."

"I have a mother who goes with her gut. She's lost a bomb. Fortunately my stepfather has several more bombs safely tucked away that he's not letting her get her hands on." The Nikkei showed a modest gain.

The finance report moved on to individual stocks and foreign exchange, and she kept watching, thinking about how soon this would all be relevant to her once again on a daily basis. She'd always found numbers and statistics and balance sheets to be good for her well-being, safe and reliable. A part of her longed to be back in her office—her clean, quiet, perfectly organized corner office, with the great coffee and the cityscape view and the hum of the heating and cooling.

But she felt a little guilty about it, at the same time, and a little anxious, in a way she hadn't been before the birth. She'd thought she had all her decisions made, but now she could see that she didn't.

She was going to need the best nanny she could find.

Well, yes, that went without saying.

But she would have to devote some serious time to conducting interviews with the candidates on offer at her chosen agency, because she couldn't leave Ben with just anyone. There was more to it than she'd considered. Maybe a trial period? Should she think about one of those nanny-cam systems? Or would it be better to have an open arrangement where she and the nanny went on Skype at regular intervals, so she and Ben could see each other? Would that work?

How was she going to leave him for ten hours every day? Her stomach dipped at the thought of it, and she snapped herself out of it. *Get a grip, Claudia.* New parents managed this all the time.

"You and your stepfather must have a lot in common," Andy was saying.

"Doesn't mean I like him much," she bit out.

Somehow, the combination of a baby on her lap, the mood of doubt about returning to work, the Chinese food in front of her and the market updates on CNN had brought on an impulsive honesty that she regretted at once. This was what they'd talked about during her labor, too. Her parents. Their divorce. Dad in Allentown. Mom and Kenneth in New York.

But she wasn't in labor now, and it was embarrassing. Made her too naked. More naked than she'd felt showing him her breast while Ben was feeding. The baby seemed to pick up on her increased tension.

No, he was just hungry after his shortened feed, starting up that fretful my-tummy-feels-wrong-and-I-don't-know-why sound that preceded a full-blown cry. Andy seemed to recognize it, too.

"Can I take him for you while you finish eating?"

They tried this for a couple of minutes, but Andy didn't smell right when Ben was hungry, and his crying only grew more frantic. Claudia stopped pretending to eat neatly and started taking big mouthfuls, shoveling it in, but it was too embarrassing, and too distressing when she knew Ben was hungrier than she was. She couldn't keep on like this.

"I'll have to leave," she finally said.

"Let me pack up the leftovers later, and I'll drop them over."

"Keep them, please." She stood and reached out for her baby, not waiting for Andy's answer. "They're yours."

"It's fine. I'll grab the stroller for you," he said. The words barely penetrated the wall of noise from Ben.

"And we can work out a couple of times for me to take him for an hour or two so you can get some rest."

From somewhere—from a lifetime ago, it felt—she summoned her spreadsheet voice. "I think he'll be fine, soon, if I have him back in our own space. We're doing great, really."

"Of course you are. You really are. But everyone needs a little time. I don't think you had much of that when Kelly was here."

"She was great. I had her friendship. That was more important than time to myself."

"Oh, sure. Seemed like you had a nice few days together, but it wasn't long."

"He's feeding well and gaining weight. My postnatal check-up was perfect. It was wonderful of you to give me dinner tonight."

"No problem."

"I appreciate it as a friend, truly I do, but there's no need for you to get involved."

At the top of the page there is faint, illegible show-through text from the reverse side.

Chapter Eight

"Andy, there is *no need* for you to get involved!" said Michael McKinley, Senior, over the phone.

"Dad, she sounded close to breaking point the last time I talked to her. That was over a month ago, and I'm a little concerned that she hasn't called since. I've called her, but she hasn't wanted to talk."

"Your sister is fine. If she can't handle the pressure, then she shouldn't be a children's cancer specialist."

"Well, then, maybe she *shouldn't* be a children's cancer specialist."

"Look, just because you've chosen the soft option doesn't mean you should push it for your siblings."

"I wouldn't dream of pushing it for MJ. He obviously gets off on the power trip and playing God, just the way you do." Andy bit his tongue. Had he gone too far? The "soft-option" thing always got to him. It wasn't the first time the accusation had been made.

He would have bought into the soft-option idea himself six or seven years ago. Back then, he was all about being superhuman, and if that occasionally meant downing a few prescription pills to keep it all together, so what? He was a doctor. He was in control.

Until one day he wasn't...

His father seemed to like the power-trip idea. "Look, you're right," he was saying, complacency honeying his voice. "I won't deny that. It's an important part of the role. I'm a heart surgeon. I have to play God. The power and responsibility go hand in hand. Your brother is putting together broken bodies day after day. It's the same for him. Scarlett needs different skills, but she has them. It would be a sheer waste if she scaled down her career out of some crazy idea that she can't cope. And if I hear any suggestion that you've pushed her into it..."

"I just think she needs some time out, that's all." Scarlett had made the time out happen for him five and a half years ago. She'd sent him up here for a weekend to a high-class bed-and-breakfast, and he'd done some serious thinking that had saved his life. He'd shifted his whole life up here on the strength of that weekend.

"Doctors don't get to have time out," his father said. "Is that a baby I hear crying?"

"It's my tenant. She's on the porch swing out front rocking her newborn, and I have the window open. She's finding it hard to get him to settle. She wants a routine, but the baby won't have a bar of it."

"Close your window."

Right. Easy. Close the window. The non-involved solution.

Andy almost laughed at his father's typical response, and at his own complicated reaction—the anger, the sense that he didn't quite belong in the high-power

McKinley family anymore, the steely thread of conviction that he was the one who'd gotten it right.

Or right for him, anyhow.

Being a family-practice specialist in rural Vermont with a file drawer full of existing patients, a waiting list for new ones, a contented set of colleagues and office staff and enough time in his life to keep fit and acquire a non-spray-on tan...

Well, that might be a soft option as far as Dad was concerned, but Andy was happy now, instead of strung out on prescription stimulants, tranquilizers and pain meds. He'd only just started out on that path, back in New York, but he would have been a lot further along it by now if he'd stayed. Criminally far.

And if overinvolvement in his personal life was a crime, too, then slap a pair of handcuffs on him right now, because he was keeping his window open and heading on out to Claudia's porch swing.

She was crying, he discovered.

Pretend he hadn't seen?

Too late. Andy had sat down carefully on the swing beside her before he noticed her red eyes and streaming cheeks, and now he was too close for pretense. They had to talk about it, they couldn't act as if everything was fine.

She gave him a watery, apologetic smile.

"You're just tired," he said.

"Yes," she agreed, but it was too fast. If she really had been crying just because she was tired, she would probably have denied it. Her tiredness underlined the fact that the whole Routine Baby thing wasn't working, and she wasn't ready to admit defeat on that front, yet.

So she was crying about something else.

She had a big damp wad of white tissues balled in her

hand, and her nose had puffed up, and the baby didn't care. He thought his mommy's shoulder was the best place in the world to snuffle and grimace and soothe himself, before the next bout of colicky pain hit. For the moment, the pain had let him go, and he was almost asleep inside the generous swathe of his fabric baby sling, his eyelids falling, his little head heavy. He was almost six weeks old, and still one of the ugliest babies Andy had ever seen.

Claudia must never, ever be allowed to know that he thought so.

"You *are* tired," he told her, "and that's why this other thing is bothering you more than it should."

There was a beat of silence while she decided whether to argue the existence of an Other Thing. Then she took a breath and said on a controlled sigh, "Nope, I think it should bother me a heck of a lot."

"Ah."

"You're right, okay? About the tiredness. About there being more than that. But this *should* bother me!" She glared at him fiercely.

"Want to talk about it?"

"My mother has cancelled. Completely. She's going to wait until I'm back in the city before she sees Ben. She thinks it would be *more sensible.* That's another five weeks."

"Only that much?" Andy murmured. Claudia's short tenancy was flying by, as far as he was concerned, but he guessed she wouldn't see it that way. Every hour of sleeplessness and stress to her probably felt like a week.

"He's so cute and adorable and *beautiful* now," she said, "and Mom is missing it. He'll change so fast! He's taking the bottle. She'd be able to have him in her arms and feed him, if she wanted. I don't want her to be 'sen-

sible' about my baby. How is it sensible for her not to
see him? He's smiling already!"

"She was planning to come up at around this time?"

"She said once he was smiling and the weather was
warmer. She gave me actual dates! I've been—" She bit
down on the next words.

Holding out for it, Andy guessed. Just so she could
get a break? Somehow that didn't seem right, didn't
seem as if it was her motivation. There was something
else she needed from her mother's visit—the visit that
now wasn't going to take place.

"What happened?"

Again, Claudia was silent for a moment. Ben was
quiet, also. She kissed the top of his rapidly thinning
toupee—actually, in this area he was definitely less
ugly—and snuggled her arms tighter around him. Andy
wasn't up with the minute-by-minute details on the routine. He guessed the baby should probably be in his bassinet or his crib at this time of the day, late afternoon,
but Claudia didn't seem to want to let him go.

From side on, he watched the way she held and
touched him, the way her face softened and her head
did that tilt that mothers did. Down and sideways, so
that whatever else was happening, she could see her
baby's face.

Her hair had fallen out of its usual knot, or else she
hadn't bothered with it today. Pregnancy and hormones
did fabulous things for a woman's hair. It was shiny and
thick and satiny, and Andy's fingers suddenly itched to
tuck it behind her ear and linger against the soft skin of
her neck.

She wore a draped and stretchy pale yellow top that
outlined the soft fullness of her breasts, and black leggings that clung snugly to her gym-toned thighs. She

hadn't lost all the pregnancy weight on her tummy yet. Probably didn't have time to try. It was brave of her to come up here, really, all on her own.

Brave, or else she hadn't thought it through.

Andy suspected the latter, but still, she was sticking it out, just as she was sticking out the sore nipples, the breast pump, the postnatal exercises he'd seen her doing on her yoga mat in the backyard. She hadn't gone rushing back to the city to hammer on the nanny agency's door.

"You know when people make four or five excuses," she finally said, "it's never as convincing as when they make just one?"

Andy had to laugh. "I've never thought about that, but I guess you're right."

"She said she had a sixty-fifth birthday party to go to, and her feet were giving her trouble, and my stepfather had a cold she didn't want to pass on, and she hasn't found the right gift for the baby yet."

"About three excuses too many?"

"Exactly. She should have stopped with the party." She was silent again, then, "And I've been totally kidding myself. I can see that now. I've been hanging on her visit, thinking she'd have some expertise and some willingness, and I'd get a break, but that was never going to happen."

"No?"

"Even if she was here, she wouldn't want to be left alone with him. She's not a big fan of sacrifice. So I'm crying—I must look horrible!—because of realizing that I should have known from the start it was never going to happen, more than I'm crying because she's not coming up. Which really doesn't make sense."

"You don't look horrible. It does make sense."

And your baby isn't ugly.

Strangely enough, all three of those statements were suddenly true. Andy kind of liked Claudia when she was vulnerable. When she was wearing a robe with her hair in a mess. When her big green eyes were puffy from tears and lack of sleep. When she treated a box of baby wipes as if they were an urgent organ delivery for a waiting transplant patient. When she was shoveling in Chinese food too fast, and then lighting up on seeing the to-his-eye-unappetizing, refrigerator-chilled leftovers the next day. When she was looking at her funny little baby as if she would be his willing slave forever.

And the baby himself was beginning to grow into his own face. Andy could see the face right now, if he looked down, just beyond his own right shoulder. There it was, all peaceful, not red and crumpled. The creamy eyelids flickered. Ben was having a dream. He smiled and it was like the glow of a candle flame, a small, quiet point of light. He was a sweet thing, a darling. You could get fond of a kid like this, even if you weren't his doting mom.

"What do you want, Claudia?" Andy asked her. "Do you want your mom to come up? Could you yell at her and make her see sense?"

"I don't want to have to yell." Another silence. "I want her to *want* to come. I've been wanting and wanting her just to call and say she was coming right away because she couldn't wait, no arguments, and she was going to take care of me and give me time out and send me shopping—I don't know what I expected. A personality transplant. She's never been like that."

The swing rocked a little. She was making the movement with her toe on the porch, pulling and pushing so that the rocking motion was just strong enough to soothe Ben. He stayed asleep, and the sling supported his weight so that Claudia could let one hand drop into her lap while the other stayed snug around his little butt.

She had gorgeous hands, well-cared-for but soft in the way they moved. Andy had noticed them from the start, and they hadn't changed, despite all the baby-bathing and diaper-changing. Every now and then, she would give Ben an unconscious caress, all curvy and graceful and slender with the fingers. She had a talent for touching.

Andy wondered if she knew it. Wondered when she'd last used it on a man.

She had a talent for swing-rocking, too. The movement made a kind of figure eight, and he relaxed into it, which nudged his body a little closer to hers. He didn't want to shift back again, in case it disturbed the baby.

Liar! He knew exactly why he didn't want to shift back.

"So what's she like, your mom?" he asked.

"Oh, what's she like? Flaky. Entitled. Beautiful. Hard-edged." There was a pause before and after each word, as if she was really trying to nail each part of the description. "She was a hippy in the late sixties when she was in her teens, rebelling against a nice middle-class background with older parents, being an only child. She dropped out of college, but then went back and did a degree in Fine Art at U Penn. That was where she met my father."

"Right. I was wondering, after what you've said about him."

"He was on a scholarship, doing applied mechanics, but he dropped out before he finished, which was a real issue for her. I don't think she could ever let it go. The fact that my dad only ran a garage..."

"Decent business."

"His hands always smelled of engine oil. I remember the way she complained, and it was true. And then her parents had to go into a nursing home, which used up any inheritance she might have gotten—they died, I don't even remember them—so she was really bitter and stressed about money."

"That can do things to people."

"It can. It sure did things to Mom. After the divorce, she moved to New York, to this tiny little studio apartment, all she could afford, and left me with Dad until she landed a decent job in a gallery on the Upper East Side. During that time she had me on weekends. That went on for two years. I actually think she set out to get herself a rich husband, working at the gallery, and it paid off. She met Kenneth there. He was buying a Dutch Old Master. Once they were married, I could have my own room, and she took me full-time."

"Took you?"

"Claimed me, I guess."

"Did you want to leave your dad?"

She was silent for a moment, then the words were reluctant. "He made it hard…for me to want to stay. He didn't communicate much. He was pretty withdrawn. I was twelve at that point, I wasn't a great judge of how he was feeling, all I knew was that it was pretty downbeat, coming home to him every night, to this dark, gloomy house where I was the only one who ever cleaned. And my mom had a beautiful apartment in New York and spent money on me every visit and said everything I wanted to hear."

"She doesn't say everything you want to hear anymore."

"Yeah, you noticed that, too."

"Have you told your dad about the baby?"

"I sent a birth announcement. He must have received it by now."

Her silence said that he hadn't called or emailed or written back.

Andy didn't know what to say. Even if he accepted that he was getting involved—sorry, Dad—he wouldn't know what to say. He'd never met her parents and now that her mom wasn't coming up, it looked as if he never would. You needed an actual relationship in place with a person if you were going to talk about each other's parents.

It wasn't a large porch swing, and he really didn't want to disturb Ben. Their shoulders were almost touching. He could have shuffled an inch or two and made contact, put his arm around her while she let her head rest against him. He could have enjoyed that elemental contrast of sweet softness with his own hardness and strength. He could have made her feel better, and taken a nice hit of illicit pleasure in the body contact at the same time.

But a woman's head on a man's shoulder was such a massive commitment, when the woman was single by choice and a new mom. It was more of a commitment than a kiss. More of a commitment than sex.

It said, "I care." It made an offer that had its foundations in the life force of the entire mammalian kingdom. All through nature, mothers with tiny, unprotected, milk-fed babies wanted a male to shoulder the load of hunting and warding off prey, during the period when they themselves were hemmed in by their maternal role.

Andy didn't normally accept his biological destiny in such terms, but in this situation it was so glaringly obvious. Claudia needed him right now, but if he responded to that need, they might both become trapped in a short-lived relationship with totally the wrong foundation that would be bound to turn ugly when it ended, as it would once her need grew less intense.

He would have risen at that moment—carefully, so as not to rock the swing too much. He would have found the right exit line and gone back into his own place, but then he saw a brown van pull up at the front of the house.

Parcel delivery.

"I'll get it," he told Claudia. He'd ordered some books on the internet a couple of days ago. Could this be them?

But the package was too bulky, after he'd signed for it and taken it, a box that looked as if it had been re-cycled and strengthened with lengths of gray tape, and it was addressed to Claudia. Big capital letters. Thick black marker. He brought it up to the porch. "For you."

"Would you mind…?" She made a movement with her elbows that pointed out the obvious. She had Ben in her arms. She couldn't even pick up the bulky card-board cube, let alone open it.

"Put it inside your front door?"

"Yes, that would be—" She stopped suddenly. "Wait, turn it around, can you?"

"Sure. Which way?"

"So I can see the sender's address."

He found it, and saw the name, Len Schmidt, before he turned that side of the box to face Claudia. "It's from Dad," she said blankly.

"I guess he did get your announcement."

"He's sent a gift." Claudia's statement of the highly obvious suggested surprise verging on shock.

"Looks that way. Let me put it—" Andy began, going

back to the previous plan of opening her front door and placing it just inside.

But things had changed, now.

"Would you open it?" she said. "I—I can't imagine what he's sent. In such a big box. I was expecting a card or a rattle. Mom hasn't even sent a gift, yet. I thought she might bring a few things when she— Yeah. Anyhow." She didn't want to talk again about the fact that her mom wasn't coming up. "I suppose this'll be a plush toy."

"Too heavy, I think." He put it beside her on the swing and she tried to tilt it with one hand, but couldn't. "You really want me to open it?"

She nodded, her cheeks pink. He was surprised at the level of her reaction, and said quickly, "Let me grab something to slice through the tape." He was back pretty fast, with kitchen scissors in his hand. Not the ideal tool, but the one he'd found first.

Even so, she'd been too impatient to wait. Her fingernails were picking at one corner of one piece of tape, even though it was such a well-taped box it would take an hour to get it open at the rate she was going. "I can't imagine what he's sent," she repeated, on a half murmur.

"So let's find out." He took one blade of the scissors, put the box on the porch and scored through the tape that covered the center opening, taking three tries to make the full cut because the scissors were too blunt. There were still two more cuts to make along each side.

Claudia sat forward, the pink spreading on her cheeks, her expectancy and curiosity and impatience so strong Andy could almost touch the emotion in the air.

Shoot, was this the first gift anyone had sent for her?

Did she project that much of an aura of separateness and self-reliance?

Andy couldn't know for sure, but he thought it might be the first. Kelly had brought a couple of things, of course, including a fairly tame group-purchased gift from a wider circle of friends, but Claudia had just let slip that there'd been nothing from her mom. Work colleagues usually put in for a gift when there was a wedding or a new baby in the picture, but maybe they were waiting until Claudia was back in the office.

"Some plush toys can be quite heavy," she murmured again. He couldn't tell if she wanted a plush toy or not. Was she steeling herself against the disappointment of a garish or poorly thought-out gift? He remembered the words she'd used earlier about her mom.

I don't know what I expected. A personality transplant?

Seemed as if she didn't know what to expect from her father, either.

Andy had cut through the layers of tape. "Okay, here we go." He opened the top flaps of the box and encountered blue tissue paper, thick layers of it. They looked recycled rather than new. "Do you want to save these?"

"Yes, I think so. Put them here." She patted the seat beside her with her free hand. The other one was wrapped around little Ben in his sling, still fast asleep.

Andy peeled off the layers of tissue, found a garment beneath, and heard Claudia hiss in a breath. It was an old-fashioned christening robe that had to be at least a hundred years old. He barely dared to touch it, looked down at his hands first, to make sure that none of the black marker pen had smeared onto his fingers when he'd handled the box.

Okay, they looked clean. He picked up the delicate

robe and held it by the tiny shoulder seams for Claudia to see. It was made of fine cotton fabric with hand embroidery and gathered ribbon, white on white, and it dated from the days when babies of both sexes wore gowns that came well beyond their little feet.

"I don't recognize that at all," Claudia said.

"It looks like a family heirloom."

"It must be. From the Schmidt side."

"How come your name's not Schmidt?"

"It used to be. We changed my last name to Nelson, my stepfather's name, after I went to live with them. I did keep Schmidt as a middle name."

"What did your dad think about that?"

There was a hesitant half shrug. "He never said."

Andy laid the christening gown on the tissue paper on the porch swing. There was more tissue still in the box. He lifted out this layer also and laid it on top of the gown. Beneath it, badly wrapped in pastel-hued teddy-bear wrapping paper, was a big, soft, squishy parcel. The paper had torn, and there was a fuzzy orange-and-white ear sticking out.

"Okay, here's the plush toy," Claudia murmured.

Andy pulled off the paper.

It was a tiger, squashed temporarily out of shape by the box, and made in realistic tiger colors. A baby tiger, Andy decided, because its face had an appealing expression, no fierce tiger growl in sight. Ben would probably love it with great enthusiasm as a toddler, until it fell apart from too much hugging. Right now, the tiger was about three times the size of the baby.

"It's cute," the baby's mom decided. "It's really sweet. Is—is there more?"

"If I take out the tiger, several more packages, I think." He lifted out the plush toy and it assumed its tiger shape as he laid it on top of the sheets of blue tissue on the swing. It was more clearly a cub now, a lying-down tiger, not a stalking or crouching or pouncing one. A sleepy baby tiger. Then he pulled out another tissue-wrapped parcel. "Something hard inside this."

"Unwrap it for me?"

He did. "Christening mug. Yours." He read the engraving out loud. "'Claudia Elizabeth Schmidt, Grace Lutheran Church, March 12, 1978.'"

"Wow." She swallowed.

"Put it with the gown?"

"Please."

There were still several items in the box, each of them swathed in bubble wrap. The outline of the celebratory bottle of champagne was recognizable but he pulled off the bubble wrap anyhow. "French. Nice brand." He sat it on the porch.

Next came some books, six or seven of them. A couple were new, beautifully illustrated children's stories from a quality bookstore, not the garish, cartoonish things that passed for kids' books on a supermarket shelf. The other four were...you'd have to call them *well-loved.*

"They must have been Dad's when he was a boy," Claudia said, on a whisper. "He saved them. Did he read these to me? I don't remember. But I was a girl, I liked fairy books and books about animals. He used to read those. Oh, how long since I've thought about that! He must have had so much patience. I wanted the same story, over and over. But he still kept the boy books, just in case. And now there's Ben. I can't believe this..."

It was strangely silent on the porch. A car swished by, and the swing creaked a little. Andy held his breath, feeling another wash of helplessness and not knowing what she needed, or what to say.

"Keep going," she told him, after a few moments.

"This I can't even work out," he said, finding the next object in the box, beneath a froth of foam pellets. It was hard and heavy, but too small to be another bottle of celebratory champagne. He had a struggle with the tape that fastened the bubble wrap in place, but finally pulled out a silver hairbrush, comb and mirror, all taped together.

"Those were mine," Claudia said. "More Schmidt heirlooms. I wasn't so keen on them at twelve, but they're...wow, they're beautiful." Andy unwound the tape holding the three items together, and gave her the brush. She put it beside her on the swing and traced the filigreed design on the silver back. "I had a different brush I took with me to stay with Mom, pink and plastic. I thought it was gorgeous then. The silver brush set just sat on my dresser. The last time I went to the city...I didn't know I wasn't coming back."

"Did your dad know?"

She pressed her lips together. "That's a question, isn't it?"

"You don't know if he knew or if he didn't?"

"Mom made it seem as if he did, at the time."

"Made it seem?"

"Led me to believe. I asked her about it a couple of times as I got older. She always insisted that Dad had to come to the city if he wanted to see me, and he did, a couple of times a year. If he protested that arrangement, I never heard. We'd go to the zoo, or for a burger. I never asked him whether he was happy about any of it. You know, you just don't. I didn't, with him. It feels so awkward. There was a wall. He wasn't...cheerful, most of the time. And I don't think kids credit their parents with normal emotions—or emotions that kids have themselves, or can relate to—until they're quite old."

"That's true, I guess."

"Mom told me, 'It worked out the way your father wanted,' and I believed her. I believed he'd known. And the second time I asked she said, 'Would you have wanted to stay with him?' and I— You know, thinking about it now, I don't think he did know."

"No?"

"I think she sprang it on him once I was safely in New York. But the thing was, it hadn't been fun, living with him, which made me think even if he had known that I wasn't coming back, that last weekend, he wouldn't have said anything, or tried to stop me leaving."

"You're right, he could have fought for you. But there's more than one reason for not doing that. It doesn't mean he didn't want you."

"I know. I've never known what to think. I just remember how miserable I was, living with him after Mom left. In my head, all the memories have gray skies, and no leaves on the trees, even though I was there with him for two summers, so that can't be right. Looks like you've reached the bottom of the box."

"Just about." Andy sifted his fingers through the foam pellets and found one last thing. "There's an envelope."

"A card?"

"Must be."

"He should have put that on top, so I'd find it first," said the efficiency expert that frequently spoke from Claudia's mouth.

"And another little package taped to the back of the

envelope," Andy said. "Your dad likes tape." He gave her the card. It had her name on the front, in the same block capitals as on the box. CLAUDIE.

She looked down at it as if she was scared of it, her expression reluctant and complicated and closed. Andy didn't know what she was feeling. He thought she probably didn't, either. "I'm going to save this," she said. "I need to think about this. About all of this. About him calling me Claudie. He always used to. No one else ever has. I'm sure Claudia was my mother's idea, as a name. Dad couldn't quite deal with it." She shook her head and stopped, as if wondering why she'd said all of that.

"Claudie is nice." Andy himself had called her Claud, a couple of times, without meaning to.

It had begun to feel chilly on the porch. The baby hadn't stirred on her shoulder in quite a while.

"I'm going to try laying him in his bassinet," she told Andy, putting the envelope on the swing beside her. She took a breath, went into professional courtesy mode. "Thank you for helping me with the package. I had no idea it would be such a task when I asked you to open it."

"No problem. Need help getting up?"

"I've got it." She steadied the swing with her free hand on the seat, and stood carefully, so as not to disturb the sleeping baby. Then she looked at the discarded bubble wrap, the tissue paper, the books, the tiger. The only thing she picked up was the card, which she held half as if it might be a bomb, half as if it was made of spun sugar or antique glass.

"Can I pack all this stuff up for you?" Andy offered.

"No, I'll put Ben down and take care of it." She kept thanking him all the way inside, card pressed in her hand, then said, "I'm fine from here, please go enjoy your evening," and so he left her, feeling weirdly disappointed that she hadn't opened the card in front of him.

Feeling as if he'd been shut out of something he was entitled to know about and be a part of.

Feeling that he knew her a whole lot better and had a whole lot more of a connection with her than he wanted.

Feeling as if the card contained something that had the power to change several lives, and both of them knew it.

After twenty minutes of switching the TV on and off, checking his email, picking up a medical journal and not taking in a word of what he read, he called one of his canoeing buddies, Ethan, and asked, "Want to go for a beer and some wings? Think we might get Chris and Vince along, too?"

Dad, I apologize for doubting your wisdom, and I will never rent the other half of my house to a new— single, beautiful—mom again.

Chapter Nine

Claudia put the champagne in the refrigerator to chill, even though she probably wouldn't find anyone to drink the lion's share of it for her until she was back in New York. She put the tiger in Ben's portable crib, where he slept during the night. This was supposed to signal to him that nights were different to days, as far as sleep went, but she didn't know if it was working. Maybe a stripey new friend would help.

She put the brush and mirror set on the dresser in the bedroom. It had taken Dad twenty-two years to send it to her. Twenty-two years. It didn't make sense.

She looked at the card in its envelope and the little taped package. Andy was right about Dad and tape. There was more tape than contents, from the feel of it. She pulled the package free and opened the envelope.

It was a baby card, nothing special. Sweet and pretty and generic blue, with the words, *Congratulations on*

Your New Baby Boy! on the front. She opened it up, and it was covered thickly in handwriting, and there was an inserted sheet of notepaper, too, as if once Dad had gotten started, he couldn't stop. Maybe that was why he'd sent the brush set. Once he'd gotten started with the gift-giving...

The strength drained out of her legs and she had to sit. Her hands were shaking and the words had blurred.

Don't cry *again, Claudia! At least read it first, before you decide it's a reason for tears!*

Dear Claudie,

    I was so happy to get your announcement about the baby. We haven't talked in a while. I've wanted to call or write, but I'm not good with that stuff and I didn't know what to say. I'm out of the habit of writing. You wouldn't think I'd been to college but then it was only eighteen months, wasn't it, and no graduation. I know you will be a great mom. A lot of women are doing it on their own these days. Men, too, for that matter. You should be proud of yourself and I hope you are, the way I am proud of you. I would love to see him if that is possible. They change so fast when they're little. You could tell me if there's a good time for me to come see you in the city, once you're back there, the way I used to. We kind of stopped doing that when you got to college age. You wouldn't have wanted to sit across from me with us not knowing what to say. I would love to hold him. There's always something to talk about with a baby. As for me I'm doing great now. Better than I was for a long time. That was my fault. There's a lot of stuff that I regret that was my fault. I let go of things and stopped trying and I don't blame your mother for leaving. It was that thing they call a self-fulfilling prophesy. I knew your mom was too good for our situation and eventually the bloom would come off the rose and I walked forward to meet that moment instead of fighting it. I knew it was a fight I couldn't win but I should have at least tried. Just like I should have tried harder with you, to be a better father, to get beyond my own problems and think about your needs. Listen to me, I didn't plan on saying all this but it's written now so maybe it was meant to be, and I'm having to find another sheet of paper. Anyhow I have a nice new lady in my life now and we are good together. No blooms on anyone's rose and we laugh about that. We have some simple good times and that is fine. We don't ask for the whole of the moon just a piece of it shining in our window. I have sent a few things as you will have seen. Some of them might come as somewhat of a surprise. That brush set and christening gown from the Schmidt side. Well I should have sent the brush set years ago but I was angry. I knew that was maybe the one thing I owned that your mother would have valued as it is real silver and antique. The christening gown was yours, I don't know if you remember from photos, but before that about ten other Schmidt babies wore it down the years. The necklace you won't know about. I bought it the weekend you didn't come back from New York. Your birthday was coming up and it was so pretty. But when your mother called to say you wanted to stay with her and could I send your things, well this was my problem again. I brooded on it and the gift never went in the mail along with the other stuff and the longer I kept it the harder it was. I didn't want to bring it when I came to see you because I was afraid of what emotions I might put on you. After your mom left I brooded a lot and I don't blame you now and I didn't blame you then for preferring to live with her. But I would love to see the baby.

Your loving father Len.

It was growing dark outside, and in the room, the pages of the card and letter had blurred to pale shapes on which the writing barely showed. In Claudia's hand, the thin silver chain with the silver sailboat charm threaded onto it had grown warm with the heat of her body. There was a little nest of tape and bubble wrap tossed on the coffee table in front of her.

Ben began to stir at last. She could hear him snuffling and moving on the monitor. How long had he slept? Nearly three hours? That had to be a record for this time of the day. It was funny, really. The one time he'd slept, and instead of sleeping herself, or taking a bath, or stretching out on the couch with a book, Claudia had just sat here, blinded with tears and frozen with emotions she couldn't even name let alone express.

Nothing her father had said about the past and his relationship with Mom surprised her. She'd filled in most of those blanks herself, over the years. She'd seen the photos, the colors of thirty-five years ago distorted and faded by the plastic film in the old albums, but the reality apparent even so. He'd been an incredibly virile and good-looking man when he and Mom had met in 1975. He was twenty-four years old and she was twenty-two, they made a stunning couple, and even in the photos you could see the magnetism between them, the deep-boned physical attraction. The bloom on the rose, Dad had called it.

He'd known it would wear off, that he wasn't the kind of man who could keep a woman like Mom forever. He didn't have the money or the style or the social standing, or even the wildness and recklessness that she channeled these days into her drinking and playing the finance markets, all he had were the looks and the blue-collar charm.

He couldn't resist her, back then, when she'd been so willing and so dizzily in love, but he was waiting for it to end—waiting with such a sense of certainty that he'd almost made it happen, and when it had, he'd retreated into himself.

"Brooding," he'd called it, and Claudia remembered. All those times coming home from school to a dark house and a cold kitchen. All those evenings when he would sit in front of the TV without a word to her, after she had made them grilled cheese sandwiches to eat, lost in shallow shows with canned laughter or implausible murder plots that she still couldn't watch in reruns because of the bleak memories they brought.

And yet the letter was so important.

I would love to see him… I would love to hold him… I would love to see the baby if that is possible.

The wistfulness of it shafted into her like an arrow. The simplicity of it, after her mother's thin excuses for not coming up here, lifted her heart. The honesty of it drew forth an honesty in herself that she couldn't ignore.

Yes, Dad, I've been angry with you, hurt and disappointed and confused. I've let our relationship dwindle away when I could have pushed harder, but you could have pushed harder, too. I don't think you're perfect. I don't suddenly think Mom is wrong about everything and you are right.

But you want to see my baby. You want to hold him. You know how fast he's going to change. You sound as if you want Ben to belong to you a little, as well as to me.

And that's important. *I want him to have someone else to belong to, and we have to make it happen. We just have to.*

Ben let out a wail on the monitor. He would need changing and he'd want a feed. It was past his bath time, according to the schedule. Should she skip the bath? But he hadn't cried the last two times, even when she was shampooing his hair. She almost thought he was starting to like the water.

She went to his room, picked him up and hugged him to her heart. "How am I going to have you meet your Grandpa, baby boy?" she whispered to him.

Allentown to Vermont was a six-hour drive. Would Dad come up if she invited him? Could she call, without bursting into tears, or saying the wrong thing? And what would Mom say if she knew the two of them were trying to mend the frayed relationship and reach out?

Plenty.

"That's not a reason, Ben," she told her baby. "Because if I listened to your grandma, you wouldn't even be here."

"Want another game?" Ethan held up his pool cue, but Andy shook his head.

"You already beat me five times, why would I want to make it six?"

"Maybe you'll show a shock return to form," Chris suggested.

"More likely I won't." They'd had a nice night, the three of them. Vince hadn't been able to make it, but three was just as good as four for a night of bar food and beer and pool. Only problem was, Andy's mental absence became more noticeable with less of a crowd.

Ethan suddenly shot a double-take at one of the booths on the far side of the room and swore under his breath. "Okay, I get you," he said. "Sorry to push."

"Wh—?" Andy was confused.

"I get why you're five down on our games, when normally the rest of us have to work as a team to bring you to your knees." He made a blunt gesture with his shoulder.

Andy turned to study the booth Ethan had been looking at, and saw Laura with her new man, Will. Judging by the empty plates in front of them, they'd finished their meal, which meant they must have been there for a while. He hadn't even seen them. Apparently Ethan and Chris hadn't spotted the pair, either, until now, but then no one would expect them to have that kind of a sixth sense about Andy's ex. He was the one who should have sensed her presence.

"It's not a problem," he told them.

Laura saw him looking in her direction. She must have been aware of him here in the bar since she came in, and she seemed angry that he hadn't been equally aware of her. She gave one of those waves where each finger comes down in turn, real slow, to suggest irony and cool. It was accompanied by a token smile and a flick of her blond hair as she turned a five-hundred-watt gaze onto Will, leaned across the table and picked up his hand.

"Okay, Laura, I get it," Andy muttered under his breath.

He was irritated. Their breakup had been, at worst, mutual. She'd been the one to leave. She was the one in a new relationship and ecstatically happy, if her deliberate body language was telling the truth. He wished her well, sincerely. So why did she act this way when their paths crossed, as they had done a few times now since the breakup?

He didn't understand it and he didn't want to think about it. He wasn't going to go over and greet her. It had always been a problem between them, this insistence of hers that the focus had to be constantly on *her* or *us,* that if he wasn't thinking about her and the relationship and her needs every minute of every day, it was a major betrayal.

It hadn't been a betrayal. He valued independence, that was all. In himself and in a woman.

"So why are you off your game?" Chris wanted to know. "Not a patient?" Chris was a doctor, also. "I saw your scoliosis kid, did some tests and measurements and she's a great candidate for surgery. I'm referring her to Feldman in New York. I think she'll have a great outcome."

"Yeah, thanks for filling me in," Andy answered absently. He snapped back into focus for a moment. "Oh, Brianna? That's great, she's a nice girl. No, it's not a patient."

"Someone, though."

"Just my tenant."

"What, not paying the rent? Dismantling engines on the carpet?"

"Baby won't stop crying."

Ethan and Chris were a gold mine of ideas, mostly involving earplugs, loud music and cutting short the lease. "Take a vacation," was the only one that remotely appealed. Andy promised to think about it, and their evening broke up as they went out to the parking lot and went their separate ways.

At home, the lights were out in Claudia's half of the house, and Andy was shocked at his level of disappointment. Had he really thought she might hear him coming up the steps and put her head out the door to tell him what was written in her father's card? Why did he care? In five weeks she'd be back in the city and he'd never see her again. He was not getting involved.

There was just no easy way of getting from eastern Pennsylvania to central Vermont, or the other way around.

Claudia had called her father this morning, to learn something he hadn't mentioned in his letter—that he'd had knee surgery two weeks ago, and wouldn't be able to travel this far for a while. If he was going to see the baby anytime soon, she and the baby had to come to him.

Now, at almost six in the evening, she sat on the porch swing with Ben asleep in his baby sling in her arms, her laptop on the swing seat beside her, a pen in her free hand and a spiral-bound notebook on her thigh. She was proud of herself for managing it.

See? If a woman put a little time and thought into being organized and efficient, she could multitask even when she had a baby who didn't do the *R*-word that those damned books were so keen on.

This didn't solve her central problem, however. To fly between here and Allentown, she would have to do so much driving to and from airports, as well as a change of aircraft, she might as well drive the whole way.

But that was six hours.

Make it eight, to allow for feeding and diaper changes and whatever else Ben might decide he needed along the way. A scenic stroll. A bath. A bare-bottomed kick on a blanket. These were the things he seemed to like way more than he liked being asleep in his crib in the dark.

Eight hours.

On her own.

With a baby.

Andy pulled into the driveway. She didn't particularly want him to find her here. Reason one, it was another piece of evidence that the by-the-books routine wasn't working. The books said nothing about porch-swing time at six o'clock. Reason two, she'd already spilled far too much to him about her complicated relationship with each of her parents. Reason three...

Ah, yes, good old familiar reason three.

He must have been at the hospital, because he was wearing scrubs with a light jacket on top so that, while at the wheel, he could pretend he wasn't. The jacket wasn't zipped. All those TV medical dramas were really onto something in the scrubs department. They looked way too good on a man with a tanned and well-honed body. They clung. They molded. They were thin, with not much more than underwear beneath.

And sometimes, after a long day, they acquired a rumpled look that reminded you of bed sheets....

He came up the steps, energetic and springy and relaxed. "Hi. Hey, he looks happy!"

"I know. This works. Go figure."

"You'll be able to write your own book."

"It'll be short."

"And you look busy." He glanced down at the laptop. "Flights?"

"More like no flights. Or three flights. Or two drives and three flights."

"What, Alaska? Iceland?"

"Allentown."

"Ah." Beneath the rumply bed-sheet scrubs, his body slowed to a standstill. "That's where your dad lives. Is he—?"

"It's fine," she said quickly. "It's good. He wants to see the baby."

"If you're going to do a tour, you could drop in to Manhattan and show him to your mom. Might work for her. Wouldn't disrupt her social life." He shook his head. "Sorry, that wasn't nice."

"It's okay."

"I had no right to judge or comment—" he seemed to be giving himself a lecture, more than apologizing to her "—just because you chose to share some of your feelings about—"

"It's fine," she cut in. "The thing is, Dad has just had knee surgery, so he can't travel this far, but he really seems to want..." Oh, shoot, she was going to cry again! How long did these hormones *last?* "*Really* to want... just...to see the baby," she finished on a husky whisper.

He said gently, "Which really makes you want to make it happen, after your mom keeping you and Ben at arm's length."

She nodded. Made herself smile. "Crazy, huh? Travel at this point wasn't in the plan at all. But his card was—" *Don't cry!*

"Is travel in the plan, now?" Andy said. "If the flights are so difficult?" He picked up the laptop and lifted the notepad from her knee, laid them both on the porch and sat down beside her. It was getting to be a habit, on his part, sharing her swing.

"I'll drive." She rocked the swing with her foot on the porch floorboards.

"He likes that," Andy commented, about the rocking.

"I'm putting it into the routine. It does seem to settle him, as long as I don't try putting him down too soon."

"Maybe he just likes being in your arms. What's the point of being a baby if you don't have warmth and body contact and love you can feel? You really going to drive?"

"It's either that, or not go. And at least if I drive I can bring everything. The baby swing. The pump."

"Or you could wait till he can come to you. Not that long…"

"Too long." *Blink, Claudia, blink!*

Too late. A big, splashy tear fell onto her hand, and he saw it.

"Talk about it," he said softly.

"This is crazy. It's the card. Letter, really. Long. It was so…just simple. After Mom. *True.* He's not the kind of person who pretends to feel what he doesn't. I might not know him that well, but I do know that. He said it three or four times. 'I'd love to see the baby.' It sounded wistful, as if he didn't feel he had the right to ask so much. He said the same thing that I've been thinking about Mom not seeing Ben."

"Yeah?"

"That babies change so fast. Like he knows what he'll miss if he doesn't meet Ben for another few months. And Mom doesn't seem to care about that. I so much want to meet him halfway. But halfway, with his knee, is Allentown."

Andy didn't answer. She sensed a building tension

in him. He couldn't stand crying, hormonal new moms a moment longer, was the problem. He'd probably already seen five of them today. "How long since you've seen him?" he eventually asked.

"Four years. I can't believe it's that long, but when I think about it…"

"That's a while."

"And even then, it was only a forty-five-minute lunch on a weekday, when he came to the city."

"When do you plan to go?"

"Tomorrow, if I can think of everything I need to pack."

"So soon? I guess with the holiday weekend…" It was Memorial Day, Monday. Her dad had pointed out the great timing. His new lady, Dorie, would be off work three days in a row.

Andy said slowly, "I have the weekend more or less free…"

"You can't. I wasn't hinting— If you mean—"

"Of course that's what I mean. Claudia, I opened that package for you yesterday. I saw how you reacted." He stood, rocking the swing, and paced the porch. "I can see how you're reacting now, just thinking about what he said in his card. At this point, I can't *not*. So go call your dad and tell him we're coming."

Chapter Ten

They had spent another ten minutes arguing about it before Claudia gave in.

She'd covered all the bases, and Andy had an answer for everything.

Yes, he could take the time off work for a four-day round trip. He didn't hold office appointments on a holiday weekend, and Tuesday was no problem. He had an arrangement with other doctors in his practice to cover for each other at short notice, whether for emergencies or scheduled hours, and he was owed.

Time to pack? How much gear did she think a man needed? Not half as much as a baby.

Accommodation? Well, was she planning on staying at her dad's house?

Claudia admitted she had no idea, and that she'd never met Dorie. It could be awkward.

So they would rent motel rooms, he said.

She heard the plural, two rooms not one, and her next question went unasked. *What's in this for you?* Whatever was in it for him, it wasn't the obvious thing, and if that little clunk in her heart was disappointment about it, then she was even more of a fool than she'd thought.

At nine-thirty on Saturday morning, fully packed and ready to go, with a clean and well-fed baby snuggled against her chest in his sling, she still didn't know what was in it for Andy, and didn't want to think about it.

He would be here at any minute. She could faintly hear him next door—a creak or two when he went up the stairs, the thump of his feet coming back down, rhythmic and energetic, as if he was taking the stairs two at a time. Right now, he might be grabbing the keys he kept in a ceramic dish on the hall side table near his front door.

Damn it! How come she knew that, about where he kept his keys?

He'd insisted on taking his car. "More leg room. Don't argue."

The whole arrangement seemed fragile on both sides. She'd begun to like him too much. Way too much. She noticed way too much about the flavor and rhythm of his life. Did he like her, or was he just the kind of man who couldn't ignore a woman in need? The timing was all wrong, the situation impossible and her judgment something she didn't trust.

She'd been so desperate last night to have a better… or safer…option than Andy, she'd called Kelly to see if she could help with the drive, maybe meet her in Allentown and do the return journey, but Kelly had unbreakable work commitments, despite the holiday weekend, and that was that. One excuse, not three.

She'd been so desperate, she'd called Dad for the second time that evening, thinking she was going to cancel, less than three hours after making the arrangement in the first place. She was going to lie. The baby was sick. One excuse.

But Dad had sounded so... Shoot, just happy. He'd told her, "I was going to call you back, too. Dorie says she can easily have the spare bedroom cleared out by tomorrow." She could hear the spark in his voice. "It's no problem at all. If you'd like that."

"That would be great, Dad."

"Your friend— Your—?"

"Andy." His name would have to do, since she wasn't even sure about "friend."

"Andy will still have to have the motel, because there's only a single bed, there isn't the room. But if you'd rather all three stay at the motel..." He was tripping over his words, keen to make sure Claudia was comfortable with the whole arrangement, that she knew she had options and the choice was hers.

"No, it would be great to stay with you," she told him. It wasn't the house of her childhood, but one very similar, a little rundown and old. She'd never been there, just seen a picture of it that he'd sent with his Christmas card one year. "And Andy might like to have some space."

"I've made a reservation. The motel is only half a mile from us. It's a good one, with room service and a heated pool. You'll both eat with us, any meal you want. Dorie loves to cook."

"Are you sure?"

"Claudie, don't, okay?"

"Okay. Thank you, Dad."

He'd never asked why she'd called him again, and the lie about her having to cancel because the baby was sick had gone unspoken. She'd barely slept between Ben waking in the night and her own keyed-up state about the visit.

She heard Andy on the porch, now, and the sound of his front door closing behind him. She opened her own door so he wouldn't need to knock, and wheeled her suitcase with a bump across the threshold.

"Ready?" he asked.

"Totally ready now, but in another ten minutes we might not be, so let's get going."

He knew enough about babies to understand what she meant. He pointed his key fob at the car waiting in the driveway. "We need to transfer Ben's seat. Is he asleep?"

"Awake but happy. And I've unlocked my car, if you could do the seat. He had a good feed, and I've packed a cooler with frozen milk. He should be ready to drift off once the car gets going. I swear, he'd sleep twelve hours at night if I could just keep driving him around."

"Someone should market a crib that has an engine hum and a sensation of movement." Andy crossed the front lawn to the second driveway.

"Oh, my gosh, that is brilliant."

"You know what, though, babies wouldn't fall for it." He disappeared into her backseat and emerged half a minute later with the baby carrier in his hands. "It's like when you give them plastic toy keys to play with. They're not fooled. They want the real keys. And they would know they weren't really in a car."

"Babies are spooky, honestly."

"They have us whipped. It's nature's way."

She laughed, and watched while he strapped the infant carrier into the back of his own vehicle. She lifted Ben out of the sling and laid him in the seat, fastening the harness across his front, while Andy loaded in the frightening amount of baby gear she was bringing.

The baby smiled at her and she smiled back, with that gooey, melty feeling that made the sleep deprivation and helplessness all seem worthwhile, and made her wonder how she was ever going to learn to leave him for hours at a time each day with a nanny she didn't even have a face or a name for yet.

Well, he'd be just that crucial couple of months older, by then, she told herself, which would make all the difference.

It was a gorgeous day. Straightening and closing the passenger door, she could hear the sound of lawn mowers in the air, and later there'd probably be the smell of barbecue, as people enjoyed the holiday weekend out of doors.

"What did you have to cancel, Andy, to do this for me?" she blurted out. "You were pretty vague about that, yesterday."

He shrugged as he loaded her suitcase into the trunk. "A visit from MJ and Alicia, with their kids, that's all."

"You cancelled your family's weekend?"

"Relax. It was just lunch." He dumped in his own duffel bag, the portable crib, and several more pieces of baby gear. "They're staying with some friends on Lake George for the weekend. They were going to drive over on Monday, then head back to the city from here."

"Lunch Monday was your whole weekend plan?"

"Well, Ethan and Vince had talked about a canoe trip or some fishing. Nothing definite. Listen, you didn't force me into this. Or nag me. So let's leave it." He slid into the driver's seat.

"Thank you." She strapped herself in beside him, stealing a glance at his face.

"Seriously." He caught her look and met it steadily.

"I know. Seriously, I'm thanking you, and now I'll leave it."

Too much silence.

His fault, probably, Andy decided. He'd come on a little too strong in not wanting her effusive gratitude or her guilt. Now he'd squashed her into a silence which left too much space for awareness.

He flipped on the radio, but it didn't help. From the four speakers—excellent quality—came the kind of 1970s rock music that was made for a fast drive along scenic roads on a sunny late-spring day. Baby Ben seemed to like it, with the volume turned down a little to soften the beat. At any rate, he wasn't making a sound.

"Is he sleeping?" he asked Ben's mom.

Claudia shifted to look around, and Andy noticed the movement too much, with too many of his senses. Every impression made him ache. The sound of her pretty outfit sliding against the seat, the scent of her perfume, the angle of her neck and jaw as she looked at Ben and answered, "Like a baby. It's a major achievement."

Andy laughed.

Claudia shifted again, settling herself deeper into the passenger seat with a shimmy of shoulders and tush. Shoot, cars were so *small!* There was no easy escape. He couldn't step away or turn his back, all he could do was watch the road as they looped and dipped beneath the green trees. It wasn't enough. He knew he was going to be deeply conscious of her body so close to his for the entire drive, and when they stopped for fuel or lunch or to change and feed the baby, it would be worse.

What had he sworn to himself less than two days ago, and so many times before that? That he wasn't getting involved? Since when did a twelve-hour round-trip and four days in each other's company count as not being involved?

Suddenly it seemed important to be merciless about his own motivations. Would he be doing this, for example, if she had brown teeth and warts on her nose? Scientists did surveys on this stuff. Beautiful women in need drew knights in shining armor the way lanterns drew moths on a summer night.

He was not falling into that trap. He was not falling for *her*.

Okay, so maybe he *would* be doing this if she had brown teeth. With a few questions already tormenting him on the subject of his relationship with his own father, her reaction to the card from her dad had reached deep into him, touched him in a way he couldn't ignore.

Damaged family bonds mattered. Andy saw it in his patients all the time. He felt a professional obligation to do what he could—suggest counseling, refer someone to the right social service, take the extra time during a routine appointment to probe a little deeper when he sensed there was more going on than high blood pressure or aching bones.

Dr. Michael James McKinley, Senior, his father, considered this to be overinvolvement, but that was just too damn bad.

I can do this, Andy thought, tightening his hands on the wheel. *I'm doing it to make the world a tiny bit of a better place, not because I have the hots for her.*

Liar!

Shoot, he was a liar, and bigheaded, and up himself, all at the same time, every bit as arrogant as Dad, only in a different way. Thinking he could make a difference, thinking he was that important—to this woman or to anyone else.

When we've finished this, I'm pulling right back, he decided. Anything else is going to be a minefield for both of us. Five weeks from Monday, her lease is up and she'll be gone. That's not long enough for me to get in too deep, even if I sleep with her.

Hell, was he planning that?

Don't lie to yourself, Andy.

Yes, he was.

Chapter Eleven

"It is so wonderful to meet you! Come in!" The round-bodied woman who must be Dad's "new lady," Dorie, enfolded Claudia in a huge hug. When she let go, she was still smiling, pink-cheeked and flustered. She had light brown salon-tinted hair, cut short, and an open face and chunky rings on several fingers. "Len is out back firing up the barbecue. He is managing great with his knee. We were starting to think you weren't going to make it."

"I'm sorry," Claudia said. "We had to stop a few times because of the baby, and then we hit traffic coming through New Jersey. We should have called, but Ben was crying at that point and I didn't think."

Ben had stopped crying now. Andy had him in the infant carrier, standing just behind Claudia. They were all squeezed into a small front hallway. Dorie was too flustered to think of moving everyone farther into the house. It was a sweet little place, nicer than it had looked in the photo Dad had sent years ago, made of clapboard and around eighty years old, still in need of some renovation but freshly painted and with big sturdy trees shading the rear yard with their fresh summer green.

"It's not a problem, honey," Dorie said. "Just glad you made it safe. Oh, he's heard you, here he is!"

He'd aged.

Well, it had been four years.

And he was in a wheelchair, temporarily, because of his knee surgery, one leg of his jeans cut away because of the bulk of the dressings still in place. She had to bend down to reach him. Their hug was more awkward than the one she'd had with Dorie. Funny how the history between two people could make a hug such a complicated thing.

"Claudie…good to see you. So good to see you." His voice came out gruff.

"Dad." He smelled of barbecue starter fluid and smoke and cotton shirt, and he was grayer and a little thinner than she'd remembered, or expected. Healthy thin, though. Ropy, as if he worked hard. Good-looking, still. Gray, but not bald. She had an inkling that Dorie was probably rather proud of having a new man with a full head of hair at her age.

There was no room here for four people plus a wheelchair and a baby. "Come through," he invited, so she ended up introducing Andy with a few awkward phrases as they trooped through the kitchen and out onto the back deck, with Dad rolling ahead of them, negotiating the doorway and the temporary ramp he'd probably put in himself, before the surgery.

My friend, she called Andy. *Well, my landlord, technically. But he was at the birth. Too hard to explain.* She mumbled and tripped over half the words, used her hands to fill in blanks or suggest the unclear status.

Dad said, "Like that for us, too, at first." He threw a loving and slightly shy glance at Dorie as he arrived at the barbecue, using an expert flick and roll to park the wheelchair side-on so he could reach the grill plate. He'd always been good with anything that had wheels. He slid some steaks onto the hot metal.

"No, I didn't mean we're—" Claudia began, but then caught Andy's frown and shake of the head.

"Don't," he muttered.

Dad and Dorie hadn't heard. "And so this is him," Dad was saying, flipping the wheelchair around again. "This is the little man."

"Yes, this is him." Claudia took the infant carrier from Andy.

"Put him on the bench," Dad said. "Will it fit, the car seat?"

"I'll take him out of it."

"Do I get to hold him?"

"Of course."

"I've forgotten how. Dorie's grandkids are in school, I never met them as babies."

"He probably needs a diaper change."

"Well, you'll have to show me. We used cloth diapers for you, and I wasn't real good at those, even then, and I never did one in a wheelchair."

"Oh, Dad, I didn't mean you had to change him!" The whole idea scared her, actually.

"Right, no, of course you didn't…" He laughed, embarrassed about his assumption.

"I was just warning you. He might not be that fresh. Hold him first, if you want, and I'll change him in a bit."

"Ah, look at the little man!"

"Isn't he beautiful?"

"He's a doll! Yes, let me hold him now before he gets fussy—does he get fussy?"

"Ohh, yeahh!"

"—and before I have to work on those steaks."

"I'll handle the steaks, Len," Andy said.

"Will you let me hold you, little man? Will you cry?" Dad held out his arms, and Claudia unstrapped Ben from his seat and nestled him into position in the wheelchair, on Dad's lap.

As usual, she had to fight back her tears. They hadn't been here five minutes, her father had every excuse to keep his distance, handicapped by his still-healing knee, and yet he was holding her baby, with the biggest smile on his face and a laugh chuckling up from his belly, and Dorie looking on as if she approved with her whole heart.

"Oh, but we haven't told them about the room, Len!" she said a moment later.

"Oh, yes, the room."

"We cleared it out…turns out there's a leak in the bathroom pipe in the wall, we didn't know about. I'd said to Len the room smelled damp."

"You had, and I didn't get to it before the surgery, thought it must be coming in the window."

"But it was so cluttered, we couldn't check. We only went to clear it out this morning and then we discovered the leak. You can't use it, Claudie, it's not fit for anyone, let alone a new baby. The plasterboard was like wet cardboard and the carpet is horrible. I'm so sorry."

"That's fine, Dorie, that's okay," Claudia said quickly.

"I didn't give you a lot of notice about coming. And I don't want you to get the wrong idea about—"

Once more she received a warning look from Andy.

"You'd probably rather be in the motel room with Andy, in any case," Dorie said. "It's not like this house is four-star luxury at the best of times."

"It's a nice place. Great deck," Andy said.

"Put it in a couple of years ago," Dad answered, then winked. "Only reason Dorie moved in with me."

"We're getting married," Dorie said quickly. "We just haven't set a date. Of course, it's not the only reason I moved in with you, Lennie!" She looked at him, arch and flirty and embarrassed, all at the same time.

"Oh, congratulations!" But Claudia's head was spinning.

Too much. Too much!

Dad had Ben on his lap like a pro, tender as anything, a delighted grandpa, it was beautiful to watch. Claudia felt a little anxious about it—no possibility of dropping him, was there?—but she pushed the feeling away, because her father's face was worth the risk. He and Dorie seemed so comfortable in their own skins together, a little fussy about the importance of the visitors, looking at each other like young lovers when the subject of marriage came up.

And Claudia, Andy and Ben were staying in a single motel room, and it hadn't occurred to Dad and Dorie that they might not want to share. And every time Claudia tried to correct their assumptions, Andy shook his head and glared.

"You need to get those onions frying, Lennie," Dorie said. "And you need to give me a turn with that baby!"

"Let me change him, first," Claudia said, reaching

to take Ben from Dad, who was clearly reluctant to let him go.

"And I can handle onions, as well as steaks," Andy said.

"The diaper bag's still in the car."

"I'll get it."

So there was another round of movement and slightly clumsy conversation, with everyone so wanting to do their best. Andy managed a mumbled few words to Claudia inside the house, after he'd handed her the diaper bag, brought in from the car. "We'll get a second room when we check in."

"We could call right now."

"Don't correct their assumptions."

"I don't want them thinking—"

But Dorie was heading in their direction, offering the best room for changing the baby.

"Easier this way, don't you think?" Andy murmured.

"Not sure how you figure that out."

"Our bedroom," Dorie announced. "If that's okay with you, Claudie. Use the bed so you don't have to bend down. I'm sorry there's nothing better." She began to lead the way down the corridor.

"It's fine." Claudia followed.

Andy said from behind, in a low mutter, "Which is better? To have them leave us pretty much alone, because they think we're already a couple? Or to have them spending the whole weekend trying to make us into a couple, because *they're* in love and *I* was at the birth?"

But when Claudia turned to reply, he'd stopped following and was turning back to go out to her father on the deck. Which was probably a good thing, because she had no idea what she would have said to him.

* * *

"Yes, we can offer you a second room. Connecting," said the woman at the motel front desk. "With a king bed."

Claudia opened her mouth to say that connecting rooms and a king bed weren't necessary, as long as they were on the same floor, but felt the slow squeeze of Andy's shoe on her toe. "That would be great," he said.

Okay, he was right. This was her accountant brain taking over. She squashed the instinctive compulsion to have everything on the correct side of the balance sheet and fully disclosed. The motel staff wouldn't know or care whether the connecting door stayed open or shut. The maids would know how many beds were slept in— that number would be two—but they could draw their own conclusions.

It was still early. They'd had such a nice evening. Layered. So full of different layers. There, she couldn't get any of it onto any kind of balance sheet.

The sense of family and welcome and accommodation of differences. All the catching up they'd done, but there would be more to come. The tangible sense that Dad and Dorie were in love, and that this was a wonderful secret they shared which others could only glimpse. The difference it made in her father, so that she found herself wanting to make up for all the lost years and build a real connection. He wasn't that morose, distant, aimless figure she remembered from her childhood and their rare meetings since.

Ben had been so good, most of the time, but he hadn't slept enough, he'd been passed around by too many willing pairs of arms, and by eight o'clock he just couldn't hold it together. "I'm sorry," Claudia had been forced to say. "If I don't get him to our motel and get him settled, I'm afraid he'll get overtired and just scream and scream."

So here they were at twenty after eight, and Andy had taken the portable crib out of its bag in the room she'd claimed as hers and was asking her, "Where do you want it?" They were generous-size rooms, each with a king-size bed, but with the connecting door open they seemed too much like part of the same space.

"Oh, by the window?" She bounced Ben on her shoulder. *Hang in there, little man, not much longer.* "Do you know how to set it up?"

"MJ and Alicia have one similar."

"Similar is not the same. The instructions—"

"Instructions are a conspiracy to rob the male of his natural instinct to construct shelter."

"You're scaring me now." She added quickly, "No, don't pull up on that bit yet."

"Have you set this up many times, may I ask?" He threw her a challenging look.

"I've set it up once, and I pulled up on that bit too soon and had to start again."

"Seriously, I have this covered." He pulled, and the whole thing collapsed.

"You're making me laugh. And Ben doesn't like me standing here laughing because he wants a feed, and I need to change him and put him in his sleep suit first."

"Do all that in the other room, while I search for my lost instincts. I'm not expecting it to take more than a half hour. Two hours, tops."

If Dad and Dorie could see us now, she thought, *teasing each other, turning the zing in the air into words.*

"Isn't it wonderful that you've found someone at this point in your life?" Dorie had whispered to her over their meal tonight, when the men weren't listening. "Seems as if it was meant to be."

He's my landlord. My landlord!

Claudia changed Ben's diaper and found one of his stretchy little suits in the bag of clothing she'd packed for him. The activity distracted him from tiredness and hunger, but by the time he was snug and fresh again, he was going beyond fretful and into distressed. She put him on her shoulder and bounced him. *Not long now, little man, just hold it together another minute or two.*

Andy came out of the other room, pausing in the doorway, and announced, "That clatter you might have just heard was not the crib collapsing again." He had the sleeves of his summer cotton sweater pushed up to the elbows, and Claudia almost expected to see a streak of grease on his cheek, after all the hard work.

"No?" she drawled. Couldn't help smiling at him. He just did that to her. Made her smile. Made her feel good.

"Well, okay, it was collapsing, but now it's up." He smiled, too, a little sheepish.

"Did you push on the sides to make sure they were locked in?" She tipped her head to one side and looked at him through her lashes, so he would know she wasn't *nagging,* exactly, just being hyper concerned about her baby's safety.

"Yes, I heard them lock in," he said patiently, tucking in the corner of his mouth so that she would know he wasn't being stubborn, exactly, just being hyper satisfied with his own performance.

"And did you push to check?" She stepped closer, rocking the baby.

"I pushed, I practically threw the thing across the room, but it stayed in shape."

"Good. They have that in the instructions. 'Throw crib across room to check sides are locked in.'"

"See, and my instincts told me to do that."

"Your instincts have done very well," she told him, exaggerating the tone of praise.

Stop flirting with him!

Ben snuffled on her shoulder, soothed by her rhythmic swaying. She'd progressed across the room, almost as far as the open connecting door where Andy stood. They were only a few feet from each other now, and she couldn't look away, even with the best baby in the world to draw her gaze. Andy had a helpless look on his face which echoed the feeling in Claudia's own heart.

Helpless.

Helpless to resist. Helpless to look away.

"Do we need to talk about this?" he asked, his voice low. He leaned into the doorway, his hand resting lightly on the painted frame. He slid it up and down, without even knowing he was doing it, and the movement looked like a caress.

Caressing paint, because he wanted to touch a woman's skin.

Claudia's skin.

She wished she was the paint.

"What is there to say?" she said. "I think we know... what we want. And what we don't."

"You're right, I guess. We do know. Is that okay?"

"Yes, as long as we both recognize it—that it would be a mistake."

"A mistake." His gaze flicked down and then up, as if he was battling with the need to look at her body. She felt the look like a stroke of heat.

"Big mistake," she repeated.

"Promises we couldn't keep?" Why did the word *promises* look like a kiss on his mouth?

"Or no promises. I don't need that, Andy. Promises, no promises, anything. I can't mess things up for Ben. I chose this. To do it on my own."

"You're saying you've completely closed that door?" His voice was like chocolate and rust, dark and soft and scratchy.

"I—I— That I'm never going to—? No, not never!"

"Good. You're made for it, Claudia. In all sorts of ways."

"I don't see how you can know that."

"I have eyes. I have a heart. That aura of efficiency and scheduling that you project, that's only a part of you, it's not the whole."

What was he saying? He was distracting her. What did his eyes and heart see? She struggled to keep up her protest. "Not *never*. But it has to be the right time. The right person. Done right."

"Of course it does. Do you think I wouldn't do it right?"

"I think *we* wouldn't. Two people wouldn't, any two people, in this situation."

"Any two people." The way he echoed her words suggested they were a long way from being just any two people.

She struggled on. "I watched my parents mess up their relationship. It took so long. There were so many months and years where I didn't know what was happening, what I was supposed to feel. Were they splitting up? Were they staying together? Did Mom have a boyfriend? Did she hate Dad? Was I staying with Dad? Who wanted me? It was the mess, and the back and forth."

"Ben's a baby. He'd never know."

"If we had a one-night stand?"

"Or a five-week stand." He swore under his breath, as if he hadn't meant to say it. She wondered if he'd meant to say any of this—the sweet cajoling, the cards on the table.

"A one-night stand would be better," she said bluntly.

"It would?"

"Because then there'd be no mess. It would cut off clean."

"You want to sleep with me just once."

She made herself say, "I don't think I want to sleep with you at all."

But she did. Oh, she did! She ached for it. Sizzled for it. Was scared of it. Roller-coaster scared. Heart-doing-back-flips scared. First-kiss-at-fifteen scared. And Andy could see it in her whole body because she couldn't hide it. Not when he was standing so close. Not when she could see in his eyes and hear in his devilish words how much he wanted it, too.

Ben was the one to make the decision. Swaying and rhythm and his mommy's shoulder weren't enough. He wanted milk and sleep, and there was only one way he had of asking.

"He needs you," Andy said, and it was a statement of truth that applied not just to this moment, but to the coming months and the coming years, and if Claudia messed up his life by messing up her own, she would never forgive herself.

Andy took a breath, brought himself under control and slid past her, close enough that she could feel his body heat. Close enough to touch, but they didn't. Claudia couldn't breathe until he'd taken another three paces and turned.

"I'll close the door," he said, "and then he won't be

disturbed if I have the TV on. You have all your stuff in there, right?"

"If you could just bring the diaper bag. It's in your bathroom."

By the time she'd settled herself and Ben in a nest of pillows on the bed, Andy had dimmed the lights for her, gone back into his room and closed the connecting door behind him.

Chapter Twelve

They had a lazy, family sort of day on Saturday, going over to Dad and Dorie's after a light breakfast at the motel. Andy wanted to help Dad with the leaking pipe in the wall, so the three able-bodied adults cleared out the spare room and pulled up the stained and sodden carpet, while Dad issued instructions and tried to do impossible things from his wheelchair.

Then, wearing one of Dad's old T-shirts that fitted a little too snugly across his broad chest and muscled arms, Andy took to the plasterboard with a sledgehammer to expose the problem plumbing. The two men made a trip to the hardware store together, with Dad successfully attempting the crutches he was allowed to use for short intervals now.

Meanwhile, Claudia hung out in the kitchen with Dorie—and Ben, when he was awake. Dorie had found the wind-up baby swing she'd used for her grandchildren, and as usual, the baby seemed to love the feel of the rocking motion.

Claudia was a little on edge about being alone with this woman, at first. Did they have anything in common, when Andy and Dad weren't around to disguise any awkwardness, and when the topic of Ben's adorableness had been covered from all possible angles of conversation, several times over?

"Len says you're an accountant?" Dorie asked tentatively, while the men were still at the store. She was making salads for lunch, and had plans for dinner, as well—spicy Mexican food from a new cookbook she'd received for her birthday.

"That's right," Claudia answered her. "Corporate finance—budgets and systems, that kind of thing." She peeled a carrot as she spoke. It was nice to be just the assistant, no responsibility.

"Do you know much about investing?" Again, it was hesitant.

"You mean the stock market?"

"Well, retirement funds. I have a little money invested. I had a friend who did a financial adviser's course in night school and she told me to put it into this fund. I feel so bad. The value is dropping hand over fist, and I didn't want to hurt her feelings by moving it, but I think I have to, or there'll be nothing left."

"Oh, dear..."

"I know. Do you mind if we talk about it? I'd really like your opinion, and your advice."

"Of course I don't mind! Tell me, what kind of a fund is it?"

They were still talking about it when Andy and Dad arrived back, with their washers and rings and bits of plastic tube. Dad overheard the tail end of the conversation, and said, "Oh, so you asked her about it, Dorie?"

"Yes, and she's been so great! I know where I'm going to put the bulk of the money. It's very secure, and Claudia says I can use Jill as my broker for a small parcel to invest in riskier options. I might lose all of that, but as long as the bigger nest egg is safe, I'd rather lose the small parcel than lose our friendship."

"Told you she'd know," Dad said. "Thank you, Claudie." He came up to her, propped his crutches under his arms, and gave her an awkward squeeze.

"Oh, Dad, it was nothing. I was happy to help. I'm so glad you felt comfortable asking about it, Dorie."

"Well, you know, it's like you don't want to ask doctors about your ailments when you meet them at parties…."

"It's different when it's family," Claudia said.

She was certain that she meant it, at the time.

"We have something we want to suggest," Dorie said on Sunday morning.

"Something we want to do," Dad added, in explanation. "A plan."

They both paused expectantly, waiting for Claudia to give them the go-ahead to outline the plan. The four of them—make that five, because you had to count Ben, sitting in his grandpa's lap making happy little baby sounds—were lazing over a weekend brunch out on the deck.

After yesterday's magnificent fare, Dorie had once again made the most delicious meal. Ham and cheese omelettes, freshly squeezed orange juice, an enormous pot of coffee and raspberry muffins still warm from the oven. It was nine o'clock, and she'd said last night before Andy, Ben and Claudia left the house to return to the motel, "Come in the morning as soon as you're ready. Just call twenty minutes ahead, so I can make sure breakfast is on the table."

"Let's hear the plan," Claudia invited.

She had to hide a yawn, after she'd spoken. There had been no question of any kind of a stand—not even one hour, let alone one night—with Andy last night. Ben had been difficult to settle and had then woken several times in the night. She'd ended up bringing him into the bed with her. How could he sleep on his own in an unfamiliar room? She understood why he hadn't been able to sleep through.

The books were in her suitcase, so they couldn't see the baby-in-the-bed disaster unfold, but she could practically hear their disapproval shouted at her through the closed suitcase zipper. But she'd slept better for the final few hours of the night, when Ben was snuggled in beside her, and she'd loved the feeling of his little body so warm and relaxed next to hers.

"Yep," Andy was saying. "Always love a plan, don't we, Claud?" Claudia hated that she knew him well enough now to hear the amusement hidden behind the words. She knew just what he thought about her need for plans. Go figure, apparently it was hereditary and Dad had it, too.

"We want to babysit," Dorie announced. "The rest of the day."

"Give you two some time," Dad explained.

Claudia was struck silent. The idea of not being with Ben for a whole day she found difficult even to imagine. Andy didn't seem to have any words, either.

"I have five grandkids," Dorie came in quickly, as if she thought Claudia didn't trust her abilities.

And do I trust her? What did I say to her just yesterday about family? I wasn't thinking of this!

"I— We can't," she said blankly. "Feeding him. What if—?"

"Honey, didn't you say he takes a bottle, and that you have all sorts of frozen milk?"

"Yes, but I haven't—"

"My daughter did it that way, with her two. I know the drill. You have your cell phone. I promise we'll call if we're the slightest bit worried about how he's doing."

"Oh, I know you will."

"And of course you can call us anytime you want, for an update."

"It's too much to ask...."

"You're not asking. We're offering," Dad said.

"We want to," Dorie insisted. "We're family."

"Of course you are...."

"You could go for a picnic somewhere, and out to dinner, or take in a movie or an art exhibit. You could go into Philly, it's only an hour." Dorie paused expectantly, so eager and sincere. Dad was sitting forward in his wheelchair, holding his breath.

Oh, shoot, Claudia was going to cry again. They really wanted to do this! They weren't just being polite. They wanted it for themselves, not just to give her a break. How could she say no?

"We'd love to have you babysit," Andy said. "Wouldn't we, Claud?"

"Yes. Oh. Yes. Of course." And when she saw the look on Dad's face, and Dorie's, she knew she couldn't have said anything else.

A half hour later, in the car, she told Andy, "See what you got us into, insisting it was easier if they thought we were a couple?" She was feeling jittery. They'd turned out of the driveway and it was scary to know that there was no Ben safe in his car carrier in the rear seat.

"See what we got out of it? A free day."

"A free day. Acting like a couple."

"A free day for you. I'm just the transport. And you saw their faces."

"I did," she admitted.

"They were so happy to be able to give it to us. They would have wanted to do it just as much if you'd been here on your own."

"I know. It was...wonderful to see."

"Where are we going, by the way?"

"I—I have no idea. I haven't even thought. Did we leave enough diapers for them?"

"Plenty. And if there's a major diaper emergency, Dorie can always go to the store. We could find somewhere for a picnic..."

"Would she know what size—?"

"She's seen that he's a little small for his age. Or how about Philly, like Dorie suggested?"

"Philly..."

He already seemed to have made up his mind, and was heading toward Interstate 476. Since Claudia couldn't think of anything else to suggest, she stayed silent, telling herself how good it would be.

Of course it would be good! Of course she needed some time out! She'd been missing the feel of a city the same way she'd been missing the market updates on the TV news. It was kind of confusing to discover that in some areas she was still the same person she'd once been, when in so many ways she felt so different. It was scary and unsettling and she didn't know how to handle it.

They reached the Interstate and Andy sped up,

taking her away from Ben at sixty-five miles an hour. The churning feeling in her stomach increased until it became nausea. She felt light-headed and sweaty and sick, feeling her pulses beat and her jaw almost vibrating against her upper teeth. It was crazy.

Crazy to be leaving her baby with her father, whom she hadn't seen in four years, and a woman she'd only just met.

Just crazy.

Terrifying.

Impossible.

Anything could happen.

"I can't do this."

"Wh—?" Andy threw her a startled look, taking his eyes off the road for a moment, and a new fear surged into her. What if he crashed the car? What if her precious baby suddenly had a mom in the hospital with broken limbs, or worse?

Her panic built higher. "We have to turn around. We have to go back. I can't do this. I can't leave him."

Andy was silent for a moment as he absorbed what she'd said, and her panic increased still more. There weren't many exits on this road, if she was remembering right. If they missed the next one, they'd be more than halfway to Philadelphia before they could turn around.

"We have to go back," she repeated, urgently.

"Claudia, he's fine. Your dad and Dorie love him to pieces already. They're going to take perfect care of him."

"The exit is coming up. Please turn around." Her mouth had gone dry.

"We have our cell phones. He's not sick. Dorie has a ton of experience."

"Please. I'm serious."

Andy risked another sideways glance at Claudia and saw how she looked. Dry-lipped and jittery and scared. "Okay," he told her quietly. They couldn't argue about it now, he realized, not at this speed, in the middle of a steady stream of traffic. "Okay, I'll take the next exit and we'll head back."

"Thank you." He heard her begin to breathe again.

They both waited out the minutes until the exit in silence. He drove carefully, sensing that she would panic more if he took it too fast, or made multiple lane changes. He could feel how tense and panicky she still was, although she was trying to hide it and to squash it down. A part of her must know that this was irrational, and totally incompatible with her plans to return to work full-time in a couple of months, but he guessed that her awareness of the irrationality and the disconnect only made the panic worse.

"Okay, back to Allentown," he said, once they were safely heading in the opposite direction on I-476. "Only fifteen minutes or so."

"Thank you," she said again.

"You want to do something closer to home, so we'll be in easy reach if your Dad calls?"

"No, I want to go back to their place."

He didn't say anything to this, just drove until he reached the exit they had to take to leave the Interstate to head onto Route 22, and then another exit onto city streets, another couple of turns. They were only a mile or two from her father's house now.

"You know this doesn't make sense, don't you?" he suggested gently, as they drove beneath the leafy trees of a quiet street.

"I—I just can't. Not yet. It would be different if I

knew Dorie better. And Dad, for that matter. If we'd built up to this more gradually."

"So we're just going to show up and say we've changed our minds?"

"I hadn't thought about that." She sat for a moment, deciding. "We can say it's my fault. I'm happy to take the full blame."

"Say that it's your fault that you don't trust them?"

"Not in those words."

"They won't hear the words, Claud, they'll hear what's under the words. Do you really want to hurt your Dad like that? And Dorie? When they've been so good? When they really want to do this for you?"

"Pull over."

"I'm planning to. Just waiting for a spot in the shade." He found one as he spoke, slowed and slid into it, killed the engine.

She sat there, staring down at her hands, and the only thing that stopped him from pulling her into his arms was that crazy word *uninvolved* that kept echoing in his head. *Stay uninvolved, Andy.*

As if.

But still he didn't touch her. This wasn't about that.

Or not yet.

"I'm such a different mother from the one I thought I'd be," she said, her voice wild with panic and doubt and emotion. "I thought I had it so totally mapped out. I seriously thought that the people who had difficult babies were the ones who brought it on themselves, the ones who didn't try hard enough. I thought I'd be this cool, sensible parent who made all the right choices because I'd thought everything through. I am so sorry about this, Andy."

"It's okay. It's okay."

"I'm shaking. Feel me."

She held out her hands and he took them in his. They were too warm, a little damp, the fingers with their pretty nails moving like scratchy little creatures against his own skin. They sent a tingle all the way up his arms and through his body. He loved her touch, her hands. And, yes, they were shaking.

He tried to capture the movement and make it go still, rubbing his thumbs over the smoothness, feeling the delicate shafts of her tendons and the satiny stretch of the skin over her knuckles. She squeezed his fingers and he kept rubbing, saying with his hands what she probably couldn't have listened to in words.

It's okay. It's okay.

"I never imagined that it was possible to be so connected to this little being that I'm this terrified—it's like vertigo or agoraphobia—to have him out of my sight." She stared without seeing—down at their joined hands, out through the front windscreen.

"It's the first time. You're not used to it, that's all."

"You're right, how am I going to go back to work? I *want* to go back to work! I'm not suddenly turning into this earth mom who's going to have seven kids and start wearing peasant skirts and baking her own bread. I like my job. I like figures and balance sheets. I like my business suits and my corner office and my tidy desk. But I don't know how I'm going to do this. I don't know why I'm having this problem."

Andy kept stroking her fingers. She'd begun to tangle hers in his, still jittery with the movements, but less shaky and sweaty now. Their closeness in the car was doing things to him that he couldn't control, and he tried to push the awareness away. It wasn't what she needed right now.

He thought he did know why she was having the problem, but he couldn't say it to her. She was too alone, that was the trouble. Not just alone as a single parent, but because she didn't have the wider support systems she needed. He could see how self-reliant she'd become, how her excellent income and career success had created an illusion in her that she could manage everything on her own, *better* on her own, because she could do it totally her way.

But things had changed, now. She needed someone else. Someone to talk to and listen to. A mom whose child-rearing instincts she trusted. A best friend with a new baby living close by. A dad for her baby. She didn't have any of that.

She had her father, but she barely knew him. And her father had Dorie, who seemed terrific, but Andy understood that in these circumstances Claudia couldn't trust her own judgment about a woman she'd only just met.

"What can we do?" she said. "You're right. Dad and Dorie would be so hurt. I can't do that. Not after the way he reached out. Not when they're both trying so hard. But I can't leave Ben there all day. I just…can't."

"So let's head back to the motel," Andy suggested. "You'll feel better about it knowing you're physically close. We won't stay away all day."

"And not driving. I'll feel safer, not driving."

"So that's a part of it? Your own safety?"

"If something happened to me… He has no one else. How can I live with that for the next twenty years?" She bent her head, staring blindly into a future full of new threats and fears. He couldn't help watching the sun on her hair, bringing out highlights of red and dark gold in the slippery dark strands.

"You won't have to live with it for that long," he told

her. "Ben will have other people. You'll build a relationship with your dad. You'll find a network of other parents and kids."

"That'll take time."

"And you have time. So that's okay."

"You're right, though, it's a huge priority now. It's not going to work with my mom. I never thought I'd be saying this—that I think Dad is going to be a way better grandparent, when my mom's the one with all the resources, and living fifteen minutes from me."

"You and Kelly will kick back into having common ground when she has a child of her own. You told me she and her husband are planning to."

"Ben's decibel level may have put that back by about six years," she managed to joke. He gave her hands another squeeze. *Proud of you, Claud, coming up with some humor, when you're feeling like this.*

"With time, you'll know that there are other people who love him, and whom he loves and trusts and knows. And he won't be a tiny, defenseless baby forever. I promise you, I am not going to let you get run over by a bus *today!*"

She shivered, and he wanted to hug those shoulders until she was all right again. "No one can make a promise like that," she said.

"I promise I will do my best to keep you safe for your baby, Claudia," he repeated, seriously.

"Thank you," she said. "For understanding."

"We'll head back to the motel."

And yet he didn't move. Their hands were still knotted together. His thumbs were still making that instinctive movement across her skin. She looked down and seemed to register the contact for the first time. Her hands went still in his.

"Have I shredded you?" she said.

"No, you've been quite gentle," he answered softly.

"Well, that's something."

"It is."

They both watched the contact. Andy stopped the movement of his thumbs, waiting for what would happen. Something. She wasn't moving away. She should be, but she wasn't, and he didn't have the power to take control of the moment, not with the way she was making him feel.

She loosened her grip and made a ring around his wrists with her thumb and middle finger, as if measuring their strength and size. Then she gripped his forearms, soft and firm at the same time. Heat shafted into him, arrowed to his groin.

Shoot, Claudia, if you keep this up...

But still he couldn't pull away.

"Thank you," she said.

"Please, don't. Don't keep saying that. You're having a hard time. How could I stand by and not listen?"

"You shouldn't be here at all. Let alone listening. Sitting in a car and— You should be fishing or canoeing or hiking up a mountain."

"How could I not be here? How can you not know one of the reasons I'm here? It's not exactly a hardship to be this close to you, Claud."

Silence. He knew what was coming, what he was going to do. She must know it, too. But still she wasn't moving away.

Uninvolved?

Who was he kidding?

He bent to her. Took his hands free of hers at last and found her mouth with his, and her hair with his fingers. Oh, her mouth! The dryness of her fear had gone, and only the trembling remained. Or maybe the trembling came from something different, now. She parted her lips, wanting this as much as he did. He heard the sigh and shudder and the little sound in her throat.

She still tasted faintly of sugar and coffee and raspberries, and her mouth felt like a raspberry, so juicy and sweet, the taste and moistness spilling against his lips. She kissed the same way she did everything, with heartfelt attention to detail. This was the kind of detail he could learn to like. The lap of her tongue, the soft, deliberate movement of her mouth, the whisper of breath, the touch of her fingers.

And, oh, her hair! It was in its usual knot, and he'd begun to like that because it meant he could see her neck, and the fine hairs that wouldn't stay in the knot. He stroked upward as he kissed her, and she leaned in to him, her shoulder nudging his, and her hands falling onto his thighs. Another arrow of heat shot between them, and he knew he couldn't stay here in the street in a parked car. They needed...

A bed.

A motel bed.

"Back to the motel," she murmured.

"Yes."

"I have to—" She stopped.

"What? Say it..."

"Feel different again."

"Different?"

"Feel like *myself*. Be me. Do something that's for me."

"Not just for you..."

"For you. Oh, yes, for you. I want to..." She put her mouth against his ear and whispered it, while her hands crawled up his thighs and underlined the message.

"Do you? *Do* you, Claud? You sure about this?" Sheesh, was he giving her a chance to rethink? Was he crazy?

"I'm a grown woman. Trust me to know what I want."

"I trust you with pretty much anything, at this point," he said, as the blood rushed through him and he went light-headed with exhilaration and need. This time, he was the one who was shaking as they drove.

Chapter Thirteen

Claudia's heart was pounding, beating in her ears and all through her body. Andy grabbed her hand as they went up the stairs, not waiting for the elevator to grind its way down from the third floor.

She'd been weak with relief when he'd turned around on the Interstate, then shattered by her understanding of how hard it was going to be to learn to let go of her darling baby enough to return to work. She was racked by the conflict between needing to be with Ben and yet not wanting to hurt her father and his new love.

And Andy had listened to her.

He'd listened to her and understood the crazy, impossible mix of feelings, and he was the only person in her life right now who had the power to make her feel that she wasn't alone, that she had someone on her side that she could talk to. He'd understood her fear about not knowing Dorie and Dad well enough. He'd understood her new sense that she had to protect her own physical safety for the sake of her child.

She'd wanted him before this, oh, yes. She'd noticed every detail of the way his clothing hugged his body, the lines that formed on his face when he smiled, the sound of his voice when he was happy or curious or concerned, the whole rhythm of his life.

But this level of wanting was different. This came from a connection she had no right to ask for or expect. And yet the connection was there, and she was as powerless to resist it as she'd been powerless to continue the drive to Philly an hour ago. Her head might know that her reactions were crazy, but her head wasn't in control.

They reached Andy's room and he had the key card already in his hand, fumbling to get it into the slot. The door opened and they almost fell on top of each other to get inside.

The maids had been here. The bed was freshly made and smooth, with its heap of snowy pillows. Andy opened the drawer in the end table beside the bed and took a couple of things out of it—handkerchief and she didn't see what else—and tossed them onto the wooden surface, then came and pulled her close, as if afraid she might change her mind if he gave her another second to think about it.

She wasn't doing that.

This was happening.

Necessary.

He felt so good. Strong and warm and familiar. More familiar than he should be. Somehow, all those little moments of seeing him in the yard, exchanging a word or two, watching him joshing with his friends, hearing his footsteps or his music faintly through the wall had attuned her to him, to the whole shape and flavor of him, as much as if they'd been sharing the same space, as well as the same roof.

When she kissed him, not his mouth…not yet…but his neck and his jaw and his closed eyes, on the way to those lips she wanted so much, it was just…*right*. Every sensation, every texture, every taste. Known and yet new. Safe and yet a heart-pumping adventure.

Oh, because her body was so different now from the body that had last made love to a man. Through her summery top, Andy's hand cupped a breast so much fuller. His hips grazed against a stomach still soft. How could it be that she didn't *want* a gym-toned and washboard-flat expanse there anymore? She kind of liked her own slight roundness and the soft give against him. She was a softer person now, all through.

He wrapped his arms around her back, flattened his hand across her butt and groaned and she pushed her body closer against him. *Feel this, Andy, tell me if you want this. It's not perfect. It's a ripe body now, a full-blown rose of a body, no longer a tight, hard bud. Do you want that?*

Seemed that he did.

He kissed her deep and long and slow, as he pulled her against his hardness. She rocked her hips, felt herself swell and grow moist with need. The heavy, dark pool of it sank deep into her stomach, anchoring her to the earth.

Oh, I want this, I want it.

"Can I strip you?" he said in her ear. She felt the breath and the heat, the deliberate tease of his lips brushing her skin.

"Please…yes…"

"Going to take it slow…"

"I like slow."

"Me, too." He found the buttons running down the center of her top and unfastened them one by one, taking his time as he'd said he would, pressing his mouth to each newly exposed bit of skin, until she was burning. He came to the lacy edge of her bra, and stopped. "Black. Wow."

"Who says they have to be white just because I'm a new mom?"

"I sure don't..."

"It unsnaps at the front."

"That is great news."

She unsnapped the fastening for him, and her breasts fell into his waiting hands. He buried his face in the deep cleft and she threw her head back and gasped as the sensitized skin tingled against his mouth and her whole body throbbed.

He took his time, aching minutes of it, as the top and the bra straps slid off her shoulders and fell away. He hooked his thumbs into the elastic waist of her stretch cropped pants and slid them down, stopping halfway down her butt and resting his hands there as if it was too good to move on. She felt herself swell against him, unbearably sensitized by the contact. "You really meant slow..."

"Slow is going to make you scream."

She kicked off her shoes and he slid her pants down to her thighs, running his fingers into the creases below her butt. He dropped to his knees and kissed her stomach, running his mouth down in a line almost to her folds, then he wrapped his arms around her and pillowed his head against her lower belly while she put her fingers in his hair and ran them through the short, slippery strands.

"I could stay like this. I could just put my tongue… But I won't. Because we said slow."

"Sl-slow." She could hardly bring out the word. "Do I get to strip you?"

"Not this time. Patience is thin."

"So unfair."

"Next time." He stood and pulled off his clothes in a few brush strokes of movement. A twist and lift of his arms, a shrug, a pull, a couple of steps. "Is that okay?"

"It's okay." She was almost gasping, wanting him back in her arms this second, but captivated by the sight of him, too. By the evidence of his need for her. By the shape of a body she'd guessed at beneath his summer T-shirts and thin scrubs, but hadn't known about for sure.

Oh, it was better.

She reached for him again and their bodies pressed together, the ridge of his erection cradled against her softened belly and her breasts full and grazing the light hair on his chest. She could feel every inch of their contact in electric detail.

"We fit," he said. "Our mouths…" He bent to kiss her. "Our bodies, all the way down."

"I want this so much…I want it now."

"Oh, yes."

He pulled her onto the bed so that she slid on top of him, her breasts heavy against him. He groaned and captured them in his hands, circled the dark nipples with the ball of his thumb, touched them lightly with his lips. She'd never loved her own breasts so much, never known how closely every nerve ending in her nipples seemed connected to her core, never felt so quickly ready to be filled.

He seemed to know it, to know that she didn't need

or want to wait, and he was more than ready himself. "Will you be angry if I tell you that I came prepared?" he said in her ear.

"No." She saw the foil packet he picked up from where it had been hidden beneath his clean handkerchief on the end table beside the bed. "I'm incredibly glad about it."

"Good… See, I do have some respect for planning."

He slid into her, a shallow, teasing stroke that quickly pulled away, before he came back and went a little deeper, still teasing, still with a retreat. "Are you planning this?" she managed.

It felt…scary…wonderful…oh!

Amazing.

Melting.

Very, very new.

"Going back to slow." He stopped and touched her breasts with his mouth again, each nipple in turn, so lightly, with a puff of warm breath. She watched his mouth hovering there, an agonizing, sizzling inch from the weight of her breast and then another soft, soft press, another slide easing deeper into her folds.

"Yes. This part might need slow," she said.

"I know, sweetheart, I know…"

"I bought you a swimsuit."

Claudia blinked. "How long was I asleep?"

"An hour."

"It was great." She stretched beneath the rumpled sheet, not thinking about the nap, but about what had preceded the nap. The slow part. The best part. The really magic, blissful part. And then the part where she'd fallen asleep with his arms around her, cupping her breasts, and his body spooned against hers.

"I didn't want to disturb you, so I went out, and saw the pool, which is heated and has a spa, and I thought you probably hadn't packed a swimsuit."

"Well, no, I didn't."

"But you should use this one." He held up the shopping bag. "Because the pool is gorgeous."

"I want to call Dad and Dorie first."

He held out her cell phone, already in his hand.

"How did you know?"

He just laughed. "I've programmed in your dad's number."

She couldn't hear any crying in the background, when Dad picked up. "Just a second," he said. "Dorie is changing his diaper, shall I put her on when she's done?"

"Or you can tell me yourself."

"He's a doll. Doesn't sleep much."

"Tell me about it!"

"But he's had a snooze or two, and he likes going for walks. He's a little action guy, he just likes being awake looking at things."

"Has he had a bottle?"

"Two bottles. Hungry little man."

"Did I leave enough?"

"Well, that's Dorie's department…" There was a pause, and a muffled sound, then Dad came back on the line. "She says you left plenty. Here, do you want to speak to her?"

"That would be nice… Dorie, how are you doing? We're just at the motel. We can be there in five minutes, if you want."

"There's no need, honey."

"Well, we'll be back soon after lunch." It was lunchtime now. "We won't stay away the whole day."

"Come back and check on him, visit with us a little while, and then go back out. For a movie and dinner, or something."

"Oh, yes, yes, we could do that," she agreed politely, not intending to follow through. Was it too quiet? Maybe Ben *should* be crying? "Dad said you'd just changed him, so he's still awake?"

"He's fine, honey. He's screwing up his little face. He'll go off to sleep again, soon."

"Well, okay, I'll let you get back to him. We won't stay out much longer. We'll see you soon. Bye-bye..."

She caught Andy's eye. He held up the store bag again, and it was a threat. They were staying away from Dad and Dorie and Ben long enough for a swim.

Five minutes. My baby is only five minutes from here.

She made herself breathe slowly, and looked at Andy, still holding the bag.

"What do you want to do for lunch?" he asked, when she'd put away the phone.

"Room service?"

"You're saying that because you think it'll be quicker than going out somewhere."

"You shouldn't be right about things so often, it's really not an appealing quality. Apparently you want to go out."

"No, I think room service sounds great. BLTs and a fruit platter?"

"Yes. Nice." Fruit platter... Nutrition...she vaguely thought.

"But my motivations for staying in aren't the same as yours."

"No?"

"I want to see you try on that swimsuit."

"Oh. Okay."

"Then I want to see you take it off."

He tossed the bag in her direction. She said blankly, a few seconds later, "It's a bikini."

"Yep. But there's a matching sarong in there, too."

She took his purchase from the bag piece by piece. Bikini top, string-sided bottom, scarflike sarong. The fabric was a gorgeous tropical print in turquoise and purple and gold that she loved on sight. But the top was *tiny*. And that wasn't even the main problem. "A woman cannot wear a bikini six weeks after she gives birth."

"Well, let's find out, shall we?" Andy suggested. "She might not have to wear it for very long…"

"Yeah, you hinted about that, earlier."

"I'm not sure that the top is going to be generous enough. You have really nice breasts at the moment."

"You seriously want me to put this on?"

"I do. While I order room service. So I know if I need to return it for a different size." He was grinning, looking totally evil and totally unashamed about it, and she went hot all over.

"Okay, I'll try it on. In the bathroom. No promises."

He just kept grinning, as if he knew her better than she knew herself. "Can't wait."

Well, he had to wait, didn't he?

She was all fingers and thumbs with the string ties, and incredibly conscious of Andy just a few seconds away, on the far side of the closed door. Still grinning? Probably.

The triangles of the top were dangerously small on the tight fullness of her breasts, but the underwire meant that they ju-u-st did the job. The bottom half was every bit as tiny, but even a granny-pants-size bikini bottom couldn't have covered the soft belly.

She tied the sarong high on her waist, with a knot

in the center, but that only made her look as if she was still pregnant, so in a moment of defiance she untied and retied, this time low on her hips with the knot at the side. She'd given birth a month and a half ago, and she was proud about that, not ashamed.

But when she went back into the bedroom, scrunching up her face, she was a little nervous about what she would see in his expression.

His eyes lit up and the grin got wider. "Wow..."

"But don't you think—?" She spread her fingers in front of her lower stomach.

"Don't say it, Claud," he growled, and came up to her, put his mouth on hers and his hands on her just-covered breasts and then slid them down to her belly, ran a finger around the sarong fabric at her waist, came up to pull at the string bow at the back of her neck. "Told you it might not stay on very long..."

The triangles peeled down and he brushed his palms over the hard, darkened nipples, saying half under his breath, "I love how big they are. I love your body so much, Claud, like this."

He didn't need to go slow with her this time. The fear she'd felt before, which he'd instinctively understood, had evaporated and she was ready for him so fast, ready for it to be a little rough and impatient on both sides. The fact that he loved her ripened body and couldn't hide it made her so aware of herself, of how different she was. All that soft curviness that women weren't supposed to want. She did want it, knowing it set him on fire.

He seemed to want to trace and explore and capture every inch of her with his hands and his mouth, and there was very quickly no question of returning the bikini and sarong to the store. She thought at one point,

*I'm never going to wear this without thinking of him...
I'm going to want to wear it, for the memories....*

She was still wearing it—half wearing it—twenty minutes later when they lay together on the bed, breathless and relaxed and tangled together as they fell back to earth. The string tie at one hip was still fastened, the sarong was bunched up around her waist and the bikini top lay across the pillow.

There was a knock at the door.

"That's lunch," Andy said.

"Oh, help..." She scrambled off the bed—he laughed at her for it—untied the sarong and wrapped it higher, knotting it in front just above her breasts.

"Why the rush?"

"It's *lunchtime*. The waiter won't expect—"

"No, because he's never seen two consenting adults in bed in the middle of the day before." He added lightly, after a beat, "Love that I can make you blush."

"You would!"

So she ate lunch in her bikini, which was a mistake, in hindsight, because then Andy made her go down to the pool. "I'm sure we had a deal."

"I don't remember any deal. You're serious about this?"

"Bought myself some trunks, too."

"Before we go back to Dad's?"

"Gotta show off my hot squeeze. Half an hour, okay? We can time it, if you want."

"You want to show me off? With this belly?"

"You're beautiful, Claudia," he said simply. "You glow." And on the strength of that, they went down to the pool.

Chapter Fourteen

"He has been a perfect little angel," Ben's not-quite-grandma said.

"I don't believe you for a second, Dorie," Claudia answered. "And if he has, then I'm jealous, because he hasn't been a perfect angel for me since he was four days old."

"Well, he did get a little fussy a couple of times, and he didn't sleep more than a two-hour stretch without waking, but he's still an angel."

"Oh, he is, isn't he?" She had to blink back tears, and was almost shaky with relief at being back with him again.

She'd had to fight not to snatch him from Dorie's arms, and had privately promised herself that there wouldn't be a movie today. They could sit on the deck in the sun, maybe take Ben for another walk in the stroller. And she and Andy would go out for dinner, if Dad and

Dorie insisted, but not somewhere fancy that would take the whole evening, just a family restaurant where they could be done and back to the baby in ninety minutes or less.

How am I going to leave him to go back to work?

The question hit her in the gut again, and she had to coach herself back to calmness and common sense. Take it bit by bit. Find the right nanny. Wean herself and her baby from each other in stages. It would be good to go out to dinner tonight, another step on the journey. She wanted to go back to work. She just hadn't expected to be so conflicted about it on such an emotional level.

"Movie?" Andy mouthed to her a little later, once they were seated on the deck with Dad and Dorie, enjoying a cool summer drink while Ben drifted off for what Claudia knew from experience at this hour would be only a short nap.

She shook her head, then saw his frown and added quickly and quietly, "Dinner, though." They were seated next to each other, and Dorie was talking to one of her children on the phone with Dad listening to one end of the conversation. This made it possible to negotiate the issue without the would-be babysitters getting involved.

"We should do the movie, too," Andy said.

"I don't want to impose on them too much. I know he was fussier than Dorie let on. They've already been so good."

"You are such a bad liar. This is not about imposing on them, is it?"

She glared at him because he was right, then took a big breath. "Okay, here's what I really think. A movie is no good, because I'm not going to switch off my phone in there. I'm just not. I have to be in contact. And people will hate us if it rings. Dinner we can bail on more easily, if we have to."

"How?"

"By skipping dessert."

"And kill my fantasy of watching you eat crème brûlée?"

"I'm willing to make the sacrifice. I am proud of myself for agreeing to dinner."

"I'm proud of you, too, but it has more to do with your bikini body…"

"You can be proud of my bikini body later."

"Is that a promise?"

"If you share my crème brûlée."

Dorie ended her call and asked them, "Have you worked out something for the rest of the day?"

"We have," Andy said. "We're not doing a movie, but dinner would be great, if you're still up for it."

"Of course we are!"

"Stay out as long as you want," Dad instructed, and Claudia almost cried—again—about this new, unexpected blessing in her life, a grandfather for her baby.

Andy woke up and looked at the red numbers on the clock beside the motel bed. It was 4:57 a.m. Something didn't feel quite right. Closing his eyes again, he rolled over in Claudia's king-size bed, wanting some contact, just a little spooning with that lush warm body of hers, before he fell back asleep. He reached out….

But the warm body beside him didn't belong to Claudia.

It was way too small for that.

It was Ben.

Andy opened his eyes. *Whoa, little fella, when did you get here?*

Claudia lay facing him, fast asleep, with her pajama top open at the front and her breast nestled against the sleeping baby's plump cheek. Ben must have had repeated wakings through the early hours, and Claudia had been so desperate to get some rest that she'd brought him into the bed.

"The books" weren't in favor of this approach—or not the books Claudia had chosen, anyhow. There were plenty of baby experts who did believe that bringing a baby into the parental bed was a valid choice, however. Andy had told some of his patients, "Do what works. Do what you're comfortable with. There are arguments both ways."

He had never needed to confront his own beliefs on the subject, until now.

I'm the one who doesn't belong here, not Ben.

The thought hit him like a punch in the gut, a lightning-fast blow, and a low one. Yes, you could share a bed all night long with a woman when you didn't know where the relationship was headed in the future, but you couldn't share a bed with her baby. That was Involvement with a capital *I*.

He could so easily grow to love this little baby, in the right circumstances, but he had to hold himself back from that kind of emotional investment. It wasn't what Claudia was asking for.

She was fast asleep, deep and peaceful, the way he'd apparently been for most of the night, since he hadn't heard the baby fussing, or been aware of Claudia getting up and coming back into the bed. There was something so perfect about the sight of her, hair all over the pillow and screening her face, breast softly curved above the matching curve of the baby's cheek.

It was a beautiful sight. It was *right,* in some elemental way that had its echoes going back thousands of years.

But he couldn't share it. He wasn't a part of it. Ben wasn't his to love. Claudia had never said or hinted or shown that she was looking for a father for her child. She'd said the opposite—that she didn't want to complicate her new role with a relationship that had no promises attached. What the hell was he doing in her bed, with a baby between them?

Slowly and carefully, he eased himself back to the far edge of the bed and slid out. He had his own perfectly good bed in the adjacent room, and he could even close the connecting door. Not all the way. He'd leave an inch, so that she'd know the closed door wasn't a statement.

Even though he knew it was.

They were heading back to Vermont this morning, after breakfast at the motel and a brief stop in at Len and Dorie's for a nice goodbye. Back home, he had to start to pull back, he *had* to, because the only other option was to get deeper in, and at some point that would be bound to turn sour, because she was leaving Vermont in just over a month.

If he was going to get out and leave everyone's emotions intact, he had to get out as soon as he could. He'd only ever intended this to be an interlude, and Claudia had seemed to feel the same. An interlude didn't include having her baby in his bed.

Lying there, it took him over an hour to get back to sleep, and he woke again at seven when he heard the kinds of sounds that told him Ben and Claudia were up for the day. She must have heard him in the bathroom, because she pushed the connecting door open a few minutes later. "I'm sorry, did Ben disturb you in the night?"

"Well, yes." Although not in the way she meant. "Just seemed like a good idea to come back to the other bed." Deliberately, he changed his tone. "So, you've gone over to the dark side, having him in with you?"

"I know." She gave a wry smile. "I'm a sleep addict. Who knew? No willpower anymore, not at that hour of the night. Do you disapprove? As a doctor?"

He was glad she'd added those last three words. They gave him permission to keep his distance. To be a doctor. "Not at all. Do what works. That's what I tell my patients. At some point in a few months, you'll be ready to work on a better sleep pattern for him, and he'll be ready to learn it. You can do it gradually, have his crib beside you with the side rail down to start, then put the rail up and move it farther away. When parents really want the baby out of the bed, ninety-five percent of the time, the baby is pretty soon out of the bed."

"That's what I figured. But I didn't know if I was kidding myself." She smiled, clearly pleased about his support and taking it at face value.

Andy felt like a fraud, and couldn't wait to get back to Vermont.

Vermont. It felt different, once they were back—from the moment they were back, after an emotional goodbye with Dad and Dorie—"We're only two hours away from New York, honey"—and a drive that had gone surprisingly smoothly.

The weekend had made some huge changes in Claudia's thinking, and Andy's house didn't seem right anymore, when it came into view as they drove down the street. She fought the feeling. She had five more weeks here.

Five weeks of sex and companionship, if she wanted it.

If Andy wanted it.

Did he?

He said to her after he'd helped her take Ben inside and unpack the gear, "I could drop over tonight, if you want."

There was something in his tone. Did he want her to say yes or no? He stood there on the porch, and the question came between them like an unwelcome visitor, keeping them from touching or showing openly what they felt. He was looking down at the letters he'd pulled from his mailbox, glancing up at her, then looking down again.

"Maybe not tonight," she said. "It was a long drive. I expect Ben will be hard to settle tonight."

"I could bring you some dinner."

The unwelcome visitor was still there, forcing a kind of politeness they shouldn't need. Claudia felt tired and unable to navigate emotions that weren't stated straight out. "You know what?" she said brightly, "I'm calling out for pizza."

"Small or large?" Loaded question.

She only hesitated for a moment. "Small." Hesitated again. Still couldn't read his face. "Is that okay?"

"It's fine." He tossed his keys in the air, caught them, found the one that opened his front door. His overnight bag sat on the mat, ready to be carried in. The pile of mail was still in his left hand. "In that case, I'll probably head out and meet the guys somewhere."

"Wings and beer?"

"Wings and beer."

"Sounds good."

They smiled at each other, and he disappeared into his half of the house, and she didn't know if they'd both just agreed to end what had started in Allentown, or if it wasn't as final as that. He was the one who'd talked about a five-week stand. She'd answered with one night. Was that still what she wanted?

"I don't know what I want, Ben," she told her baby, and it was such a scary thing, scarier to say it out loud in a big, silent room, because she always knew what she wanted, and this level of doubt and uncertainty felt very, very new.

She called Kelly and told her about Allentown—well, about the Dad and Dorie part of it. "Allentown is what, a two-hour drive from Manhattan?" Kelly said.

"About that. Bit longer in traffic."

"This could really work for you. Your dad could take Ben for a whole weekend. Wow, I'm jealous! Eager babysitters!"

"You can't be jealous. You don't even have a baby, yet."

"Well, about that… Richie and I have some news."

"You're *pregnant?*"

"Did the test this morning."

"You're pregnant so soon!"

"I know." She sounded happy and embarrassed at the same time. "Ahead of schedule. We got careless in Aruba. But now I'm thinking that my parents are in California and Richie's are in Florida, and it was weird, you know, having to make a long-distance call to tell them they're going to be grandparents. I never thought I'd feel the miles like that. We have no family anywhere close. It must have been wonderful, finding that your dad and his lady friend are so keen to be involved."

"It *was* wonderful. It was…a great weekend all round."

But I can't even imagine leaving Ben with them overnight.

How am I going to go back to work...?
She thought about it all week.

But she thought about Andy even more.

He had to put in extra hours in his medical practice, covering for the doctor who'd covered for him over the extended weekend, so she barely saw him. She found a note from him pushed under her door on Wednesday, apologizing about it, explaining that he would be on call three nights in a row, so he "might not be around much."

And he wasn't.

She heard him coming and going at strange hours, then heard him talking on the phone through his open living-room window on Friday afternoon, while she was sitting on the porch swing with Ben, thinking about her future.

"How far apart are they, Lisa?" He sounded very focused, full of authority. There was a pause. "Yes, I think you should head to the hospital right away, and I'll meet you there as soon as I can. Just stay calm, we'll see if we can head this off, see what's going on."

Four hours later, at dusk, he came home again when she'd put Ben in his crib and was once again seated on the swing with the baby monitor beside her, thinking about the decision she needed to make.

"You delivered a baby?" she asked, for something to say.

He was still wearing scrubs with a white T-shirt beneath. They looked clean and fresh, not the same ones he'd been wearing when he left the house, as if something had happened at the hospital that had given him the need to change.

And he looked a little wary about her question. She was sorry she'd asked it, since he hadn't caught the intent, which was to confirm their connection, not to intrude where she didn't belong. "How did you know?" he asked.

"I couldn't help overhearing when you were on the phone before you left. You weren't gone all that long."

"Yeah. It came fast." But he didn't look happy.

"Not a good delivery?"

He gave a reluctant shrug. "It happens, sometimes. There were...problems." She understood that he couldn't talk about it, with his obligation as a doctor to protect the patient's privacy. "I'm wiped," he finished. "Sorry."

Sorry I'm being distant, sorry I'm on edge, sorry I can't tell you about my work.

Which? All three?

"It's okay," she said. "You can't help being tired."

"I'm really sorry I haven't been around."

"Again, you can't help it, and you don't need to apologize." She was a New Yorker. She knew about stepping back and staying cool, so that the other person wouldn't think you were coming on dangerously strong.

Andy looked at the swing, as if considering the possibility of sitting down, sharing some time. He seemed conflicted about it, pulled in two directions at once, just as she was. He shifted on his feet, looked at his front door, looked at her and gave a smile that could have gone either way—embarrassed and reluctant, or starting to slow burn.

They couldn't go on like this. She couldn't stay on in Vermont, thinking too much about Andy, when there was so much to deal with in the city before she went back to work.

The decision was made.

She took a breath, stood up before she knew she was going to make a move. "Andy, I've decided to cut short my lease and head back to New York."

"Oh. Right." The shifting of his feet stopped. He leaned a hand against one of the porch's supporting posts and looked at her, waiting for something more. The awkwardness was jagged in the air, and they were standing too close for this.

Or maybe not close enough.

"I'll pay the full rent, obviously," she said quickly.

"Look, there's no need to—"

She pushed the words away with her hand flattened in the air. "Please let's not get distracted over money."

"We can talk about that later," he agreed.

"Can I tell you why I need to do this?"

"Of course you can."

"I've realized that the time has come," she said. "Last weekend, not being able to leave Ben, making you turn back from Philly, panicking so much. I need to learn to be away from him and trust other people with him. I need to find the right nanny ahead of time, so she's familiar with the routine—"

"Is it really about the routine? I thought you were over that a little." He straightened and took a step closer.

"No, of course it's not about the routine! Okay, it's so I can make sure she loves Ben enough, and that I can trust her enough to leave him with her. *She*. This she I haven't even met yet is going to be taking care of my baby for hours and hours every day. I hadn't thought during the pregnancy about how *important* that is."

"Because you hadn't met Ben yet, either."

"I hadn't. And now it's unthinkable that two months ago I didn't love him like this. I have to decide whether to…I don't know…put in security cameras. I need to practice leaving him in short stretches—"

"And then come home unexpectedly to check the nanny out."

"All of that, and I don't care if you think that's controlling and weird."

"It's a little controlling and weird, but I understand." He understood too damned much, she felt.

"I need to start my life. My new life. In New York. With my baby."

"You think you shouldn't have come up here? Had the baby here?" His voice had softened. How had they gotten this close? She could see the light in his eyes, the dark sheen of stubble on his chin. The eyes were narrowed a little, as if, like her, he was trying to guard against betraying too much. Their connection hadn't disappeared. She just knew she had to keep her priorities in place.

"No, I think that was great," she said. "But now I'm just marking time. And scaring myself about the nanny. Scaring myself, period. I need to be in my own home. My sublet ends this weekend. I'll head back to the city on Monday."

He swore under his breath, then narrowed his eyes and pressed his lips together.

"What?" she asked, almost angry about it.

"It's okay. Doesn't matter."

"I'm thinking it does."

"All right, then…I don't want you to go." He reached out and curved his hand against her neck.

Now she was definitely angry. With him. With herself. There were promises contained in those words and that touch, but she wasn't in the right place in her life to hear promises from him and he wasn't in the right place to make them, and they both knew it. "Please don't say that!"

He wrapped his arms loosely around her and looked

into her face. "No, I shouldn't say it. You're right. But do you want me to lie?"

"Of course I don't."

"No. And you pushed. So I said it. It's a feeling, Claudia, not a decision, or a plea. I don't want you to go. I really, really don't want you to go so soon. But I understand why you have to."

"Stop understanding. Because it's not helping."

"And do what?"

"I don't know." She pushed her forehead against his shoulder, so caught and stuck and messed up. She was so tempted to think that giving in to this would solve everything, but it wouldn't. Sure, Ben had already taught her that you couldn't set your plans in stone, but this plan—the one about going back to the work she loved, keeping the future secure for her baby and herself—wasn't something to set aside on a whim.

Yet she couldn't let him go.

His body made her melt the moment she touched it. The scrubs smelled like a laundry room, linty and lemony and warm. She could stay like this. She could just *stay* like this, all safe in his arms, hungry about it, wanting him so much, cherishing the illusion that the rightness of being in his arms meant that everything else was right, too, but it wasn't.

She had Ben.

She needed to put Ben first.

Oh, but that was abstract and a little way off in the future, a whole three days off in the future, when she would pack the car and drive down to the city.

"Talk to me," she said, standing in the circle of his arms, not wanting to move, listening to his breathing.

"About what?"

"About how it worked for you, leaving the city and

coming to Vermont. Why did you do it? I feel as if my whole life has changed and I don't know what I want, and you must have known what you wanted, to come up here, when every other member of your family is a hotshot doc in the city. How did it happen? How did you make that decision?"

"How?" He stayed silent for a moment. "I crashed my car."

"You crashed—?"

"I wasn't hurt beyond a few bruises. Didn't hurt anyone else. Incredibly lucky. Just scraped the whole side of the car against a light pole out on Long Island, driving to a friend's beach house for a weekend at two in the morning, after I'd done forty-eight hours on call."

"You shouldn't have been driving."

"I shouldn't have taken the pills before I started the drive that were supposed to keep me going."

"There must have been consequences. A doctor. That's bad."

"I had Scarlett in the car with me. The car was still drivable."

"Did she know about the pills?"

"Not until afterward. I told her, standing there beside the road, both of us in shock. She took the wheel. We never reported it or claimed on the insurance, but she kept the keys."

"The whole weekend?"

"For three months. It was like I was under house arrest and she was my ankle bracelet. She made sure I stayed clean. Then she sent me up here for a weekend and told me to think about my life, and I didn't make the decision to move here right away, but it started a whole chain of ideas…and fears. I knew something had to change."

"And you made it happen."

"I had to. I owe a lot to my sister for it. I started with working out the person I didn't want to be, and ended up knowing what needed to happen to be the person I did."

"You didn't have a child."

"I didn't have a child," he agreed.

Not a lot more to say. She needed to think about a few things first. Not that she could really think all that clearly now...

Andy cupped her bottom with his hands and she pressed against him, feeling the way they fitted together, the way her softened belly cradled the erection he didn't try to hide. They didn't move. Moving would be a decision, yes or no. She couldn't make the decision yet and it seemed as if neither could he.

His cheek came to rest against the top of her head. He began to stroke her bottom, so lightly and slowly, as if they had all the time in the world and he couldn't help himself. She felt her nipples harden against his chest and turned her head to the side to lay it more deeply and comfortably against his shoulder. His warm neck was in kissing distance and her lips formed themselves into the right shape because she couldn't stop them.

He gave a little shudder at the soft press. She kept kissing him, loving the satiny heat of his skin, the familiar, clean smell of him. He tilted his head, seared his mouth across hers then pulled it away and drew in a ragged breath. "Hell, Claud... What is this? Last fling?"

"I—I think so." She found his mouth again, and this time he deepened the kiss until it reached every nerve ending in her body.

"You sure?" It came out raw, from deep in his throat, his mouth a fraction of an inch from hers.

"If I wasn't sure, I should have said no last weekend," she whispered.

"You can still say no now." He pulled back.

"Do you want me to?"

"No. Hell, no! *Hell,* no!" The words came on a dark mutter. He was looking for her mouth again. Clumsily, now, as if it was dark and he couldn't see. She looked at his face and found that he had his eyes closed and tight, his face in a grimace as if he was still fighting this.

She ran her fingers down his back, rested them in the same place on his body that he was using on hers—that tight, yummy butt of his, covered in just two thin layers of fabric. They were locked so tightly together, it was indecent, out on the porch, only half screened from the street by a shrub or two.

But she still couldn't move.

He began to slide his lower belly against her, side to side. Just an inch each way. Rolling himself. I want you, his body said. I want you. Her body answered back, hips tilting, moving like an exotic dancer with a glittery costume slung low on her belly. The strength flooded out of her legs and she could barely stand.

"Come inside," he muttered, tightening his hold. He must have sensed the cooked-spaghetti feeling in her limbs. He bent and grabbed the baby monitor to give her, then picked her up, holding her thighs until she wrapped her legs around his waist and her arms around his neck. He carried her as if she weighed as much as Ben's plush tiger. She felt as if she did—light and empty of everything but her need.

"Where?" he demanded, after his door was closed behind them.

"Anywhere…"

He went for the stairs and finally let her feet to the ground. They stumbled up together to his room, keeping contact, while she still had the baby monitor in her free hand. She felt that if she let go of him, she might change her mind, and she didn't want to change her mind. She wanted this.

They paused on the landing and he covered her with his hands. Everywhere. Rediscovering all the things he'd learned about her body last weekend. She loved that he needed to do it, that he wasn't taking her body for granted. There was a sense of wonder and preciousness in the way he touched her, the places he lingered, the things that made his breathing change.

In his room, they undressed with clumsy speed and fell to the bed. He pulled her on top of him, cupping her breasts, running his hands down her back, ready to enter her as soon as she wanted.

Which was now.

Because if she waited, paused, or even talked, she might not let this happen. The sensible part of her might get in the way, and she didn't want it to. Not this time.

Oh, close your eyes, Claudia, don't let yourself think. Just feel.

She rode him, arching her back upwards, squeezing him tight, loving the way he filled her. His hot hands anchored her backside and he groaned and bucked when her breasts brushed against his mouth and her hips rocked with his.

His climax chased hers, caught up and overtook and they were both crying out at the same time, lost in each other, their bodies so tightly locked together she forgot who she was.

Afterward, he fell into a doze, but she lay there wide

awake, listening to the impossible contradiction of sounds—the abandonment of his deep, relaxed breathing and the snuffles beginning to sound on the monitor, coming from Ben's room just through the wall.

Chapter Fifteen

It was a crazy weekend, Andy decided.

They made love as if the world was ending on Monday, and they barely talked. When they did, it was only about immediate things—what they wanted to eat, whether they'd take a shower separately or together, when he was likely to be back home after being called into the hospital to see a patient, whether Ben would stay asleep much longer.

Andy didn't know what was happening. Maybe he didn't want to know. Maybe he just wanted the sex.

But the sex didn't change anything. Sunday night, after they'd grazed on cheese and olives and cold cuts and crusty bread in front of Claudia's open fire, she told him, with a tight expression, "Andy, I need some time by myself in my own bed, if I'm going to make the drive to Manhattan tomorrow and get Ben properly settled in."

You're still going to make the drive?

But he didn't say it out loud. What difference did it make, really, if she left tomorrow or in four weeks when her lease was officially up?

"Have you heard anything about the sublet?" he asked, instead.

"I had an agency handling it. They phoned while you were at the hospital. The tenant has moved out, the place has been cleaned, and everything's in order. I think the guy broke one wineglass, but that was about it."

"So you're all set."

"I'm all set."

"I have to work in the morning. Do you want me to help with anything before I go?"

"It's fine. I'll try to make an early start, but if it takes me forty minutes to load the car, it's not a problem."

"Well, if I see you…"

She sort of smiled. "I'll let you fold down the crib. Since you're so masculine with that."

"I hate goodbyes."

"Me, too. So shall we not?" Again, that stiff little smile, and the tense shoulders.

"Not say it?"

"Not make it into a big deal. This is goodbye, now. I'm waving at you, see? I'm saying thank you for everything. And you're walking toward the front door."

He wasn't.

Not yet.

But he had to.

He stood slowly. Was this really what they both wanted? It was way harder than it should be. "Doesn't have to be goodbye, Claud…"

She looked at him with that tight face. "It does."

"Because this wasn't in the plan?"

She nodded, just one little jerky dip of her chin.

And it would be crazy to argue with her, so he didn't, he just let himself out and into his own place three steps away. It felt horrible and wrong, down to his bones.

He heard her in the morning, moving around next door, heard the front door opening and closing and the trunk of her car slamming shut. Stealing a look from his front window, he saw her make another trip to the car, with Ben's portable crib folded away in its carry-bag. She had her free arm flung out sideways to balance the weight, and her shoes looked too flimsily attached to her feet for all those trips up and down the steps. They'd talked about him helping her to pack, but he held back.

All that would do will be to create the need for a second difficult goodbye, and he wasn't sure he could go through it again.

When he came home from work that afternoon, he discovered that her car was already gone, and she'd left the keys to the house in an envelope that she'd slid between the porch screen door and the frame.

Nice while it lasted, Andy, but now it's over.

Putting out the trash a little later, he discovered something else—a carton of paper sitting beside his recycling can. Atop a pile of newspapers and computer printouts, there was a stack of baby-care books with authoritative, impossibly optimistic titles and dog-eared corners.

"She's thrown 'em out," he muttered to himself. "I don't believe it!"

A small, warm flame kindled inside him and he found himself grinning. She wasn't still poring over them. She wasn't even passing them on to some other desperate, and possibly deluded new mom with spit-up on her shoulder. She considered them worthy only of being sent to a factory and turned into cardboard.

"Good for you, Claud."

Good for him, too, maybe?

For some reason, he couldn't get those discarded books out of his head.

"Welcome home, Ben," Claudia said to her baby and the empty room.

Even though she'd made an early start, she had needed to make several stops to take care of the baby, so it was after three in the afternoon when she pushed open the door of her apartment and brought Ben inside.

It didn't feel like home, at first. She opened the sliding door to the tiny balcony and in came a blast of city air and noise. There was a breeze to lessen the heat and a distant glimpse of the Hudson River and Riverside Park. The low roar of traffic was punctuated by horn blasts and sirens, and went quickly from seeming alien to being familiar.

She liked it. She liked the energy of it. She liked the echoing resonance made by the deep canyons of the streets running between the tall buildings. Kids who grew up in the city had a self-reliance and an open outlook that she thought made up for the things they missed. The sense of community was different in the city, but it was still there.

And her apartment was gorgeous, furnished carefully over the past five years with classic pieces, restful colors, a high-quality Turkish carpet and a collection of Art Deco glass.

"What do you think, Ben?"

But Ben hadn't yet made up his mind.

She switched on the coffeemaker, and the rich aroma began to defeat the sense of unfamiliarity. This really was home.

She spent over an hour with Ben in his sling across her chest, or laid briefly on a blanket on the floor while she fiddled around, hanging fresh towels in the bathroom, making her bed, bringing the rest of her things from the car parked in the garage beneath the building. This took eight laborious trips, because she didn't feel safe leaving Ben alone in the apartment for the time it took to descend twenty-six floors in the elevator and come twenty-six floors back up.

It was home, but there were challenges here, now, that she hadn't experienced before.

She thought about Andy and felt a sharp and already familiar stab of loss which she hated because of the weakness it betrayed. She'd chosen to do this on her own. How Mom would jeer at her for such a rapid crumbling of her independence and certainty!

"Shall we call up your grandma, Ben?" she asked the baby.

But he needed a feed and a change and a nap. Calling anyone at this point was out of the question. An hour later, at almost six in the evening, he'd fallen asleep on her breast and she could ease him away from her body and lay him on the couch in a nest of pillows. The books wouldn't be happy. Too bad. She'd left those behind, and the satisfied, victorious feeling she'd had when they thumped down into that carton beside Andy's recycling can still seemed like a celebration.

She picked up the phone but didn't call her mother. She called the nanny agency, instead, leaving a message on their voice mail. "Hi, it's Claudia Nelson. We spoke a couple of months ago. You have all my details on file. I'm ready to arrange some interviews for a full-time position. If you could call me back first thing in the morning."

* * *

"Thought I should call you to tell you my rental ended early and the place is free for you anytime you want it," Andy told his sister's voice mail on Tuesday. "Call me back so we can talk dates, and get something settled."

Scarlett didn't call back, so he left another message three days later. This time she did phone, but he had his cell phone switched off while he was seeing patients, so again there was no direct contact, just more voice mail.

"I'm sorry, Andy, I can't make a decision about it right now," she said. "Don't put off any rentals for my sake. I don't think it's going to happen. I'm sorry to have messed you around. I should never have suggested it. Just forget it, okay? Hope we can talk soon. Bye."

"You're going to have to move once he's mobile, or that balcony will be a death trap," Claudia's mother said.

"I'll keep the sliding door locked."

Mom wasn't convinced. She continued her tour of the apartment, seeming to relish every opportunity to point out a safety issue or an inconvenience or a sign of how Claudia's life had changed for the worse, her trim, well-dressed figure moving about like a curious bird. She'd asked about wine and had shrugged when Claudia said there wasn't any. "No problem."

But Claudia wondered if her mother's restlessness and carping would have lessened if she'd had a drink in her hand. Or would it only have been worse?

"Bet you never thought your gorgeous furnishings would have to jostle for space with a crib and a change table and a baby gym." Mom laughed huskily. "And isn't there somewhere else you can put the stroller so it's less in the way?" She nudged the stroller wheel with her foot, trying to make it squeeze more tightly into a corner near the door.

"Well, I'm using it so much. We walk in the park at least once a day." Claudia had been back in the city for five days, and this was Mom's first visit. She'd come laden with expensive gifts and had said all the right things in the first five minutes. Ben was beautiful. He looked so healthy and strong. Claudia had her figure back amazingly fast.

Then they'd kicked over into minute number six and the tone had changed and finally Claudia burst out, "I can't work it out, Mom. Do you enjoy the idea that I might be stuffing this up, or are you genuinely hoping that your criticisms might help me learn?"

Mom's eyes widened. "It's bringing back the memories, that's all."

"From when I was a baby?"

"I thought I'd go crazy! Hellfire, I remember! You think you'll never get through it, never sleep or shower in peace again."

"I'm not going crazy."

"No, because you're planning to start back at work in a few weeks, so it'll be the poor nanny going crazy, instead."

"I'm not having a crazy nanny."

"Then you'd better give her plenty of time off. Will she be living in? Sharing the baby's bedroom?"

"I don't know. I haven't finished with the interviews. Some of them are looking to live in, some of them aren't."

"It would be crowded with a second adult in this apartment..."

Claudia pressed her lips together and didn't reply.

* * *

"I'm calling about the rental. Your listing says you're open to flexible lease periods?"

"That's right," Andy said to the female voice on the phone. "How long were you thinking?" He was still holding out hope that his sister would come up, and didn't want to close off the option for her, despite the apparent finality of her message last week.

"I'm hoping for a six-month lease to start, with the option to extend on a month-by-month basis. We've just moved to the area and are looking to purchase, but we need to sell our other house first." The woman explained her situation in more detail than Andy needed, which gave him time to realize that he really didn't want this rental, no matter how long it was or when it started.

It was ten days since Claudia had left, and the other half of his house had been silent and empty since. He'd had the place professionally cleaned but it really hadn't been necessary. She'd left it in perfect condition. The recycling had gone out to the curb. The cleaning company had found just one item she'd left behind, a half-used container of baby wipes that she'd forgotten about in the bathroom cabinet.

It said too much about his state of mind that he'd seriously considered calling her to ask if she wanted the box of wipes put in the mail. He remembered how he'd had to drive her to Kelly in a state of emergency with the wipes in her hand that time, because she was so panicky about Kelly taking Ben.

"...so we'd be willing to start with three months if that works better for you," the woman was saying. "But we wouldn't want to go any shorter than that for the initial lease period."

"I'm sorry," Andy heard himself say. "The place isn't available for the period you want."

It wasn't true, but still he couldn't think about having the place rented again. He'd managed to speak to Scarlett in person, but she'd told him, "Dad thinks it's a mistake."

"But what do you think, Scarlett?"

"I don't see how I can do it…"

"That's not an answer."

"No. I guess it's not."

Was it really just because of Scarlett that he didn't want another rental right now? Or was it because he couldn't stand the idea of having people next door who weren't Claudia and Ben?

"Then I don't understand why you have the place advertised," the woman said. "You should have said something right away. This has been a wasted call. You really need to keep your listing up to date."

"I'm sorry," Andy said again, and heard a frustrated sigh and the click of a disconnected call, which was probably better than he deserved.

The woman was right. He should keep the listing up to date. And he should either push his sister for a commitment or let her find her own solution to the burnout that colored her voice more starkly every time they spoke. She'd helped him when their positions were reversed five and a half years ago, but apparently she wasn't going to let him return the favor.

As for Claudia, that was done now. That was over. They'd both agreed on it, for all sorts of good reasons, and it was the only thing that made sense. He couldn't understand why he still felt so messed up about the whole thing, why there was still this tiny flame inside him, insisting on its own existence, telling him something could change.

He called his parents and told them he was coming for a visit as soon as he could clear his schedule. And if fifty percent of the reason for his planned trip was to sort things out with Scarlett face-to-face, the other fifty percent was not.

"Manhattan's a big place, Andy," he coached himself. "What's going to happen? What are you going to make happen?"

He had no answers for himself, other than his father's familiar message. "Don't get involved."

In the movies and on TV, whenever anyone conducted nanny interviews, they went one of three ways. Either there was a parade of disastrously unsuitable candidates, or there was Fran Drescher, or there was someone too good to be true.

For Claudia, the reality was different. After she'd considered eight candidates, her short list came down to two. Number one, an older Dominican woman, Maria-Rosa Herrera, with grown children, who seemed warm and genuine and didn't want to live in, but was a little weary on her feet and didn't speak much English. Number two, an Irish girl of nineteen named Katie Kelly who had five younger siblings, an energetic manner and good references from a previous job, but who did want to live in and who just seemed a little too casual about the whole thing.

Claudia agonized for three days, wished she had someone—someone like Andy—to talk to about it, finally chose Maria-Rosa and called the agency, only to be told that Mrs. Herrera had already accepted another position. At which point, Katie Kelly immediately

seemed way less desirable and Claudia beat herself up
for not snatching Mrs. Herrera on the spot.

Had Katie smiled at Ben at all? He'd been asleep at
the time. The girl had looked at him briefly in his crib—
"What a darling baby boy!"—but had she *smiled?*

Still, when Claudia took Ben into the office to show
him off and receive the adorable outfit the staff had pur-
chased as a gift, she told her colleagues, "I have a nanny
starting on Monday, and I think she's going to be great."
Because what else could she do? She'd picked the best
available applicant from the best agency in New York
City.

She ordered a nanny cam that same afternoon, and
then wondered if she should call Kelly for her opinion
on the ethics and wisdom of such a step. This panicky
state was supposed to ebb away now that she was back
in the city, putting her plans in place. "I won't call her,"
she decided. "It's not fair."

An hour later, she gave in and picked up the phone,
but reached Richie, instead. "She can't come to the
phone right now, Claudia, I'm sorry. She's in the bathroom. Again. The morning sickness has kicked in. Is
there anything you can think of to help with that?"

"Oh, Richie, I'm sorry. I didn't get sick much with
Ben." Was it really possible that, at the time, she'd con-
gratulated herself about this, thinking she could take
the credit? "People say dry crackers…"

"Yeah, we know about the crackers." His gloomy
tone told her the crackers weren't helping and she ended
the call a minute or two later, feeling that she and Kelly
were too far apart in their experiences right now to be
any help to each other. Opposite sides of the fence.
Before Baby and After Baby. Single Mom and Mom-
to-Be with a doting dad on hand. Two different worlds.

Who else could she call? Dad and Dorie? She would be too ashamed to admit to them that she was even considering a nanny cam. Mom? No prize for knowing in advance what a mistake that would be.

Once again, she could only think of one person, and that was Andy, and it scared her to realize how much she wanted him still in her life, when he wasn't in the plan and she was already way too close to throwing the plan out the window.

Somehow, Andy's mother turned his weekend visit to New York into the reason for a family lunch on Saturday, catered in. It was a tribute to both Mom's organizational skills and her role in the family that everyone showed up, even though half of the guest list were doctors.

MJ announced that he was on call, and Scarlett and their father both said they needed to swing by the hospital later on to check on a couple of patients. But still they were here.

Andy knew that he was the goof-off in the group. His mom put her years of nursing experience into volunteer work for a major children's charity. MJ's wife, Alicia, shopped and tanned and went to the salon as if beauty maintenance was a full-time job, and the kids themselves... Well, at four and two, they seemed to have more energy than all the adults combined.

Andy felt a strange and increasingly familiar twist inside him as he watched Abby and her little brother, Tyler, playing with a wooden train set and some blocks on the floor while the adults talked over appetizers and drinks.

Claudia's little Ben would be ready for this kind of play in another six months or so. He would sit on the floor with a carefully straight back and a wobbly little head, chewing on a rusk while he watched the big kids.

Six months further on, he'd be crawling around knocking down stacks of blocks, picking up a toy train and trying to make it roll over the carpet. A year after that, and he'd be at the age that Tyler was now, talking in sentences that only his mom could make sense of, not understanding or accepting that sometimes, for certain activities, he was still "too little."

This was the problem with being a family-practice specialist. Andy knew all about developmental stages. He probably had a clearer picture in his head of what Ben would be like than Claudia did. And he missed both of them, in a gut-aching, physically frustrating, emotionally wrenching and constant way that didn't seem to be easing in the slightest as the days went by. And that little flicker of flame still burned.

Claudia and Ben were here in Manhattan, diagonally across the Park. He had her home and work addresses, and all three of her phone numbers. She'd left two different business cards in the envelope with the keys. He couldn't interpret it as an especially personal gesture. It was practical, that was all, the kind of thing she would always do in such a situation—include her contact details, in case there were any loose ends.

If Andy knew Claudia as he thought he did, and respected her as she deserved to be respected, then he had to accept that she was serious about her life and about what she wanted. Didn't he? *Did* he?

What about the pile of baby-care books in the recycling, that spoke of how much a person could change? What about that flame?

"Twenty-eight hours in surgery," MJ was saying to their father. "It was a marathon but we put him back together. He'll break the alarms when he goes through airport security, with all the metal we had to put in him."

Alicia, who was gorgeously dressed, manicured and made-up as usual, passed a platter of appetizers under MJ's nose but he waved it away without looking at her, while Dad launched into a recent hospital war story of his own, clearly designed to make MJ's heroic stint of surgery seem tame.

Tyler's diaper needed changing. Alicia made a face. "He's later with potty training than Abby was." Mom offered to do it, and whisked the little boy away, leaving Alicia to answer a series of questions from Abby about a possible late-summer vacation.

"No, we're not going to France, honey, Daddy has too much work."

Scarlett took over handing around the platter of appetizers, but then put them down on an end table and seemed to forget about them. She sat beside Andy with one little finger in her mouth and when she brought her hand away a minute later, he saw she'd ripped the nail with her teeth to leave a strip of raw skin so tender it was actually bleeding.

She saw Andy looking and flushed. "I pick on my little fingers, for some reason," she said. "The rest are fine."

She held up her fingers and showed him eight manicured crescents and two tortured stubs, and he drawled, "Wow, only two," and then felt bad because she needed help, not censure. "Scarlett, you have to take some time off. I know it's Dad who keeps talking you out of it. Don't you think you should—?"

"We can eat," Mom announced before he could finish, and there was a bustle of activity as the food was brought from kitchen to table.

After a hectic meal, one he didn't particularly enjoy, he ended up with Dad in the kitchen, holding an extremely nap-ready Tyler in his arms while Dad put a half-empty wine bottle in the refrigerator. He said to his father, "Have you seen how Scarlett's biting her nails?"

"She stopped that for years."

"But she's started again." Tyler wiped a dirty face on Andy's shoulder, leaving a ketchup-colored smear on the fabric. Where were Alicia and MJ? They'd made moves to go home for their little boy's nap, but nothing had happened yet.

"Andy, as vices go, nail-biting is pretty harmless, don't you think?"

"I think it's part of an escalating situation that I don't like. She admitted she'd been having those headaches. I think she needs me. She's spoken to me more than once about taking some time off and coming up to Vermont, but you keep talking her out of it, I'm guessing, and now she's apparently talked herself out of it, too."

"Tyler?" he heard Alicia call.

"He's in the kitchen with me," he called back.

"I don't know why you have this need to see yourself as a rescuer," Dad said, lowering his voice as his daughter-in-law arrived in the room. "What will you do with your sister in Vermont, when she's bored and under-stimulated after a week of vacation?"

"Oops, he's filthy, he'll ruin my dress," Alicia said. She stepped back and took away the arms she'd held out for her son. "Tyler, walk for Mommy, okay? Mommy has a pretty dress on, and you have ketchup on your sweater."

But Tyler wanted to be carried, ketchup or no ketchup, and began to cry, stretching out his arms. "Where's MJ?" Alicia muttered. "We should have brought Maura." Their latest nanny, Andy guessed. He kept the little boy in his arms and thought of Ben and Claudia and nannies and raising kids in Manhattan. The little flame flickered inside him again.

Dad took no notice of Tyler, Alicia or the ketchup stains, but lowered his voice a little more. "You're encouraging weakness and dependency, and that's not doing her any favors. The problem with you, Andy, is that you're a soft touch for needy women and it doesn't—"

"I don't think I am, Dad. You're always saying that to me. I've bought into the idea, in the past, but I think you're wrong."

Claudia, for example. Needy? Or way too good at being independent? Way too serious about plans?

"—but when they cling to you—which they do, because you've encouraged it—"

Well, if I did encourage it, it didn't work, because Claudia has gone, and she hasn't called...

"—you feel suffocated and you back off and all they know how to do is cling tighter." Tyler clung tighter, crying in Andy's ear. "Tell me that's not what happened with Laura."

Laura? I never felt like this with Laura. Laura and I were just wrong.

Out loud, he was goaded to reply to his father, "Leave Laura out of this. And to compare her with Scarlett, in her current situation—"

"Okay, your sister is a different case," Dad conceded.

"She's not a case!"

And Claudia is not a case. Claudia is—

"But the underlying problem on your side is the same, and I've said it over and over. You get too involved."

Claudia is just across the Park, and I can't let her

just walk out of my life lugging a portable crib and never see her again, just because falling in love wasn't in her plan or mine. It's crazy. And it's not about respecting her boundaries, it's about protecting mine, the way I did with Laura, and I don't want to protect my boundaries that way anymore.

"No, Dad," he said, with finality. "The problem is that I don't get involved enough."

Chapter Sixteen

"And then twenty minutes ago—two o'clock on a Saturday afternoon!—I had a phone call to say she's decided not to stay in the city after all." Claudia pressed the phone to her ear, pacing the apartment and trying to remember to breathe.

She'd called Dad's number in desperation—she needed *someone* to talk to about this—and Dorie had picked up, and even though she felt it was unfair to be downloading on her father's partner like this, the words came tumbling out.

"And she said she wanted to tell me right away, and directly, not through the agency, 'because I know I'm letting you down,' so now I'm back to square one. And it wasn't as if I'd especially warmed to her, but I'm wondering if that's me, if I'm not going to warm to *anyone*, no matter how perfect they seem, because basically I don't want to leave Ben on his own with a stranger, especially one who might not have the right support systems in this city, because I'm starting to understand how hard that can be."

"Ah, honey…" Dorie said, and clicked her tongue in sympathy. After a moment's pause, she said carefully, "Have you talked about it with Andy?"

"No, I haven't."

"Ohh…"

"I— We're— I don't want to talk about that."

"I'm sorry to pry."

"You didn't, Dorie. It's okay. It's…complicated."

"About caring for Ben, does it have to be a nanny?"

"What's my alternative? I need to go back to work. I want to."

"I know that, but maybe you'd feel better about a child-care center? You'd probably find one close to your building."

"An actual center?"

"One that takes them from infants to five years."

"Yes, I know what you mean. But I always thought… nannies cost more. They're supposed to be better. When people can afford a nanny in New York, they have a nanny." She'd *always* assumed she would have a nanny. That was always the plan. She'd seen fleets of them walking in the Park with babies in strollers and toddlers in hand. Now she could see the inflexibility in her own thinking, could practically feel the gears grinding in her head, opening unexpected windows.

"If you can find exactly the right person, a nanny might be better," Dorie was saying thoughtfully, "but if you're having trouble finding someone you can trust, if you're imagining all sorts of things happening because it's just Ben and the nanny on her own—"

"Oh, that is exactly what I'm imagining!"

"—then you might feel more comfortable leaving him in a place where there's more supervision, and more pairs of hands. Someone who can step in if he's crying a lot and his carer needs a break."

"I hadn't thought of that. At all. My plan and my budget were always geared toward a nanny. But I—I just never thought it would be so hard to leave him."

"Plans can change. Sometimes you have no choice but to change them! One thing about having a baby, it's never how you thought it would be."

Claudia laughed. "So I'm starting to learn. Thank you, Dorie. I'll think about it. I'll do some research. Thank you."

"Anytime you need to talk about anything, honey, you can call, okay? I'm glad to have had something to suggest, when you were so helpful about my problem with Jill and the investments."

"Oh, I was happy to be able to help."

But there was no one to help with Claudia's errands, after she'd put down the phone. She opened up the stroller, settled Ben into it, found her shopping list and left the apartment, wondering how much of a time window she had before he started getting hungry and tired...

Andy heard Claudia before he saw her. Or rather, he heard Ben. A few strides later they came into view, but Claudia hadn't seen him, yet.

Him or the flowers or the cute little hat he'd bought for Ben on impulse, on the way between his parents' apartment and here.

She held the baby on her hip with an arm curved around him for support, but he wasn't happy. The two of them stood in front of the apartment building's bank of

mailboxes, which were built into an alcove just beyond
the security desk in the lobby.

The man at the desk had begun to look at Andy with
some suspicion. He needed to announce himself and
sign in, it seemed. "I'm here for Claudia Nelson," he
said, and gestured toward the alcove.

The man nodded but wasn't fully satisfied, yet. Andy
knew he was still being watched as he walked toward
the alcove. Claudia still hadn't seen or heard him. She
was struggling to get her mailbox key into the slot,
while Ben cried. She had the folded stroller propped
uncomfortably against her leg and three bags of shopping on the floor beside her. She wore a pink skirt and
top, and shoes with beads on, and dangling earrings and
looked so bright and pretty...and stressed.

"Claudia..."

At last she turned. Almost dropped her key. Took a
step and stumbled against the block-shaped shopping
bag that contained a box of diapers. "Andy..."

He couldn't find the right words. Another resident
entered the mailbox alcove, an elderly woman who only
wanted to check her box and leave. She seemed impatient with Claudia's entourage of stroller and bags and
baby, and Claudia and Andy both ended up apologizing to her before they'd found any words beyond each
other's names. The stroller fell over with a crash, and the
elderly lady left the alcove muttering under her breath,
with a native-born New Yorker's impatience and accent.

Andy didn't know how to do this. Didn't know what
to do with the flowers. They were pink, like her clothes.
Claudia looked at them in his hands, saw the little blue
sailor hat tucked into the swathe of paper and looked up
at him.

Time to commit. What was he asking? What did he want?

Claudia wanted to know as much as Andy did. Her green eyes flashed with questions and happiness and doubt.

"I miss you too much," he said, because it was the thing he was most certain of. "And I miss Ben. I couldn't let it go."

"I miss you, too. All the time. Every minute."

The man behind the desk had left his post for a tour of the lobby. "Everything okay here, Miz Nelson?" he asked Claudia, appearing at the alcove entry.

"Y-yes, fine. Everything's fine." She didn't take her eyes from Andy's face.

Ben had stopped crying now that Claudia had given up her struggle to manage stroller and shopping and mailbox key all at the same time. He yawned, and Claudia pressed his little head gently against her shoulder with a cradling hand.

"This wasn't how I planned it," Andy said. He couldn't take his eyes from her face, either.

"Did you plan it?" She smiled. She knew he wasn't much into plans.

"Not really," he confessed. "I got as far as the flowers and the hat. And you. And missing you. And not wanting to let you go."

"It's healthy that you didn't plan."

"Yeah?"

"Very healthy that I think so, right?"

"Definitely."

"And I love the hat..."

Do you love me, *Claud?*

They were really smiling at each other, now.

One of the elevators pinged to signal its arrival at

ground level and a young woman wearing black strode out in a typical New York hurry. She came over to the alcove. Did *everyone* in this building check their mail in the middle of a Saturday afternoon? She looked at them sideways and half hid a grin. Flowers and baby and stroller and shopping, and two people looking harried and stressed and radiantly happy at the same time.

"Sorry, I'm almost done," she murmured, and slipped past them into the lobby, on her way out of the building.

Andy dropped the flowers and the hat onto the folded stroller lying on the floor. "I want you and Ben in my life, Claudia. I'm not going to sacrifice what we have for the sake of a plan." He pulled her into his arms without giving her a chance to object—but, wow, she didn't look anything like objecting—and Ben looked at him with big, thoughtful eyes.

"I don't want that, either. I hate it. That we let plans get in the way, when I left." She shook her head. "And yet...I'm in New York. You're in Vermont. We have *lives.*"

"I don't care," he told her, growing in certainty with every second that passed. "Those things are not impossible obstacles. I won't let them be obstacles. I completely don't care. I just miss you too much to let you go, and that's where we start from, and where we end up. Anything else, I really, totally don't care."

Claudia could see that he didn't. There was a charge of energy and determination in him that made her crazily happy inside, made her body sing, even while her head threatened to burst with all the unanswered questions.

Sam from the desk patrolled past once more. "You sure everything's okay, Miz Nelson?"

"It really is, Sam," she said. "Just...reworking the

schedule." When he'd left again, she demanded of Andy, "Explain to me how it's going to work."

"I don't know."

"So—"

"Yet," he emphasized. "I don't know, yet. But we're two intelligent people, we can think about it. There are choices. All I know is that we have to make it work, because to turn our backs on this just because it doesn't fit with what you planned... I can't, Claud. I won't." He pressed his forehead against hers. "I won't," he repeated, and it was like a promise and a vow.

"No," she whispered, and made the same vow back to him. "I won't, either." She saw the light flame in his eyes and knew that they'd reached the point where there was no going back.

"Ever," he said.

"Ever."

"So we start with this—with feeling like this, with refusing to let it go, with wanting to be together—and we make it happen. Somehow. We don't have to make all of the decisions now. We don't have to make any decisions now. We just start with this."

"Start with this..."

"Start with me kissing you...like this..." His mouth brushed hers, deepened the contact, tore reluctantly away. "Proceed to carrying all of this stuff upstairs to your apartment." With one arm still around her and Ben, he picked up the stroller, hung the shopping bags over the handles and carried it from the alcove.

"I hope you like my apartment." She pressed the elevator button. "Because I do. I like my corner office, too."

"All we have in Vermont is corner offices, did you know that? We don't have any of the other kind."

"How is that possible?"

"Because we have space. And views." The elevator door slid open. "So every office feels like it's a corner office. And almost everyone is on partnership track, too."

"And again, how is that possible?"

"Because businesses tend to be small, at least to start. You know, Ben and Jerry were CEOs from their very first scoop of ice cream. Vermont is good that way."

"Vermont is good lots of ways. It's very good. But so is New York."

"I have nothing against New York. I'm from here, remember? I love to visit. My parents live right across the Park."

"You left." The elevator swooped upward.

"Which proves it's possible. And I told you why I left. It saved my life. But that was then. It's also possible to come back."

"Would you come back?"

"If that seemed like the best plan."

"I thought we didn't like plans."

"We like flexible plans. Shared plans. Plans we take time to work out, but that we're open to changing later on. Plans that don't control us. Plans that enhance our lives. Don't we?"

"Yes." She was laughing now. "Oh, yes! We love those."

"Plans we sometimes make on the fly. Like, maybe you could work part-time, and spend half the week in Vermont? Or you could look at starting your own practice there? Or we could find somewhere new, in commuting distance of the city? We can *talk* about this, Claudia! You have no idea how much I like talking to you."

"You're actually better at plans than you've let on, do you know that?" And she loved his vision and his optimism.

"So can I plan to take you to bed within the next hour or two?"

"You can definitely do that!" The elevator reached the twenty-sixth floor.

"And can I plan to kiss you again right now?"

"Don't plan it, just do it."

"Nope, gotta plan it, because I want to wait until we're inside your apartment. Kissing you tends to have consequences that can't happen in a public place."

"This corridor is pretty quiet."

"Not quiet enough." But he kissed her anyhow, a teasing, juicy plum of a kiss, right on her mouth, and they were both so happy, it hurt.

They reached her door. She unlocked it, and Andy practically threw the stroller inside. Ben had gone quiet, distracted by the activity. Happy to see Andy? It almost looked that way. For now.

"I don't think he's going to last much longer," Claudia warned.

"That's okay. We'll work with the window we have. We're flexible, remember?"

"We're very, very open," she agreed. "Because we know things don't always go to plan. And it's actually better when they don't. Plans can close too many doors."

"Only one door I'm interested in closing right now." He kicked it shut. "And maybe we don't have too much time in the next hour, but if you look at it another way, we have all the time in the world...."

* * * * *

HEART & HOME

Heartwarming romances where love can
happen right when you least expect it.

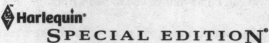

COMING NEXT MONTH
AVAILABLE MARCH 27, 2012

You can find more information on upcoming Harlequin® titles,
free excerpts and more at www.HarlequinInsideRomance.com.

HSECNM0312

REQUEST YOUR FREE BOOKS!

2 FREE NOVELS PLUS 2 FREE GIFTS!

♦ Harlequin®

SPECIAL EDITION

Life, Love & Family

YES! Please send me 2 FREE Harlequin® Special Edition novels and my 2 FREE gifts (gifts are worth about $10). After receiving them, if I don't wish to receive any more books, I can return the shipping statement marked "cancel." If I don't cancel, I will receive 6 brand-new novels every month and be billed just $4.49 per book in the U.S. or $5.24 per book in Canada. That's a saving of at least 14% off the cover price! It's quite a bargain! Shipping and handling is just 50¢ per book in the U.S. and 75¢ per book in Canada.* I understand that accepting the 2 free books and gifts places me under no obligation to buy anything. I can always return a shipment and cancel at any time. Even if I never buy another book, the two free books and gifts are mine to keep forever.

235/335 HDN FEGF

Name	(PLEASE PRINT)

Address	Apt. #

City	State/Prov.	Zip/Postal Code

Signature (if under 18, a parent or guardian must sign)

Mail to the **Reader Service:**
IN U.S.A.: P.O. Box 1867, Buffalo, NY 14240-1867
IN CANADA: P.O. Box 609, Fort Erie, Ontario L2A 5X3

Not valid for current subscribers to Harlequin Special Edition books.

Want to try two free books from another line?
Call 1-800-873-8635 or visit www.ReaderService.com.

* Terms and prices subject to change without notice. Prices do not include applicable taxes. Sales tax applicable in N.Y. Canadian residents will be charged applicable taxes. Offer not valid in Quebec. This offer is limited to one order per household. All orders subject to credit approval. Credit or debit balances in a customer's account(s) may be offset by any other outstanding balance owed by or to the customer. Please allow 4 to 6 weeks for delivery. Offer available while quantities last.

Your Privacy—The Reader Service is committed to protecting your privacy. Our Privacy Policy is available online at www.ReaderService.com or upon request from the Reader Service.

We make a portion of our mailing list available to reputable third parties that offer products we believe may interest you. If you prefer that we not exchange your name with third parties, or if you wish to clarify or modify your communication preferences, please visit us at www.ReaderService.com/consumerschoice or write to us at Reader Service Preference Service, P.O. Box 9062, Buffalo, NY 14269. Include your complete name and address.

Taft Bowman knew he'd ruined any chance he'd had for happiness with Laura Pendleton when he drove her away years ago...and into the arms of another man, thousands of miles away. Now she was back, a widow with two small children...and despite himself, he was starting to believe in second chances.

Harlequin Special® Edition® presents a new installment in USA TODAY *bestselling author RaeAnne Thayne's miniseries,* THE COWBOYS OF COLD CREEK.

Enjoy a sneak peek of A COLD CREEK REUNION

Available April 2012 from Harlequin® Special Edition®

A younger woman stood there, and from this distance he had only a strange impression, as though she was somehow standing on an island of calm amid the chaos of the scene, the flashing lights of the emergency vehicles, shouts between his crew members, the excited buzz of the crowd.

And then the woman turned and he just about tripped over a snaking fire hose somebody shouldn't have left there.

Laura.

He froze, and for the first time in fifteen years as a firefighter, he forgot about the incident, his mission, just what the hell he was doing here.

Laura.

Ten years. He hadn't seen her in all that time, since the week before their wedding when she had given him back his ring and left town. Not just town. She had left the whole damn country, as if she couldn't run far enough to get away from him.

Some part of him desperately wanted to think he had made some kind of mistake. It couldn't be her. That was just some other slender woman with a long sweep of honey-blond hair and big, blue, unforgettable eyes. But no. It was definitely Laura. Sweet and lovely.

Not his.

He was going to have to go over there and talk to her. He didn't want to. He wanted to stand there and pretend he hadn't seen her. But he was the fire chief. He couldn't hide out just because he had a painful history with the daughter of the property owner.

Sometimes he hated his job.

Will Taft and Laura be able to make the years recede...or is the gulf between them too broad to ever cross?

Find out in
A COLD CREEK REUNION
Available April 2012 from Harlequin® Special Edition®
wherever books are sold.

Celebrate the 30th anniversary
of Harlequin® Special Edition® with a bonus story
included in each Special Edition® book in April!

HSEEXP0412